i

Stolen Wealth

Don Allen

ISBN: 979-8-9883175-5-5

eISBN: 979-8-9883175-4-8

Publisher: Don Allen

Also, by Don Allen

1 Chloe

Sparks are going to fly today. Recently Sarah, my significant other, mentioned that she and Chloe were thinking about opening a business together, a private investigative service. Sarah is a retired FBI agent. She was assigned to a security detail protecting my daughter Wanda when we first met a lifetime ago. This was just after my son-in-law was gunned down on the street by the New York mob. Jeffery had flipped and was providing the FBI information on the mob's money transactions. But back to Chloe.

Chloe works for my employer, Colonel Bill Anderson, at Eyeball, Inc. Chloe is Anderson's top cyber investigator. While attending college, she had some less-than-stellar friends. They were busted for hard drugs; Chloe was with them but not using. Nevertheless, she was charged with a drug offense. This charge kept her from her dream job with the FBI as a criminal forensic analyst. Chloe's father, a member of Anderson's extensive network of friends, asked him to intercede. Being unsuccessful, Anderson offered Chloe a job with his new company doing similar work. Chloe's skills became evident over the years, earning the respect of the FBI analyst at Quantico with whom we frequently worked.

Me, I'm Sean Murphy. I'm a retired Army Ranger. I've worked for my old commanding officer, Colonel Anderson, for the past decade at Eyeball, Inc. Eyeball is one of those Washington DC Beltway firms, but in this case, located just north of Richmond. Eyeball provides unspecified services to the nation's alphabet agencies where deniability is desirable. During this time, I've been on the FBI's wanted list, targeted by North Korean agents, taken down a drug kingpin, been a Sheriff, posed as a doctor, disrupted a Mafia money laundering operation, and saved a presidential election. Oh, and also stopped a Mideast terrorist threat against the country in my free time. Throughout it all, Chloe provided timely and reliable support.

It's Monday morning, and Anderson has called an all-hands meeting. Adam, his number two, was at the front of the room with Chloe. Next to them was Butch, one of my three 'rottweilers.' Henry, the second rottweiler, was absent. He was working on a case with Lucinda, one of the FBI's criminal forensic analysts. The third rottweiler was Mark, who, with his wife Rebecca, had opened a PI agency, 'You Lose Them, We Find Them' in Lakeview, Oregon.

"Good morning. It's nice to see so many cheerful faces," said Anderson. "There have been rumors swirling around about Chloe leaving … they're true. Sean's girlfriend is poaching her!"

He lets that settle in and then continues, "And I fully support Sarah and Chloe in their new endeavor. They plan to set up an operation similar to Mark's, in Northern Virginia. I don't see this as a loss for Eyeball but rather as an expansion. As you all know, we get many requests for services that we can't respond to. Many of these requests don't require the level of response we normally provide. Sarah and Chloe have suggested they can take on some of this work, much like Mark did for us last year."

"Chloe, I have a little something for you," Anderson says as he hands her an envelope. "This will help you and Sarah set up your business. As I previously told Mark, Eyeball's resources are always available to him. I make the same offer to you."

Chloe, a bit choked up, "Thank you Colonel for your support. Without you, I don't know where I'd be. Caroline, you're now in charge of our, of your lab," Chloe tells her assistant. "I am only a phone call away if you have any questions. And one word of advice, don't let Lucinda intimidate you."

Later I'm sitting in Anderson's office with my signature mug of coffee in hand. My suggestion to Anderson's secretary that she restock the pantry with the Argentine coffee I discovered a few years ago had not fallen on deaf ears.

"What are their plans?" Anderson asks. "Name of their enterprise? Where will they set up shop?"

"They have a lead on office space in Arlington, not far from the Pentagon," I answered. "As for a name, it's still open."

"What are Henry and Lucinda working on? I haven't been able to get any sense out of him since he moved in with her," I asked.

"He's working on a project under our FBI contract with them. The project deals with child trafficking and is nicknamed 'Stolen Youth' according to Agent Wainwright," said Anderson.

Agent Wainwright, Jacob, and I go back many years. Jacob is the new Crime Division Head since Agent Dillion's assassination.

"Apparently, there are senior Mexican cartel members embedded here in Northern Virginia channeling migrant children into slavery-like conditions. Why? Do you want part of it?"

3

"No. With Sarah setting up a new business, someone has to stay home to watch Sparkles." Sparkles is the small beagle Sarah 'rescued' from some street thugs last year.

2 Gonzales

I have a condo in a small community on the north side of Richmond, ten minutes down the road from Eyeball. Sarah, on the other hand, has a real house in Alexandria's trendy Delray neighborhood. It's a 1930s vintage Craftsman Home, beautifully maintained with matching landscaping. This weekend we are vegging out in her living room, watching a Netflix series about some high-priced lawyers. Sparkles snuggled in between us on the sofa.

"Well, what are you and Chloe going to name your business," I asked.

"We haven't decided yet; a name will come to us in time. We have leased some space in a refurbished warehouse over by Potomac Yards. It's about five minutes from here and is squeezed between Route 1 and the train tracks."

"Sounds like a lovely area," I said.

"Actually, we got a great deal. A five-year lease for two thousand square feet in a fully modernized facility in a part of Northern

Virginia that is being yuppified. It's located between Alexandria and Arlington and has dedicated parking spaces."

"We're putting signage up Monday. You can come over and supervise," she said with a smile that I interpreted as 'you show up, we'll kill you.'

And of course I was forced to drive by Monday afternoon. Large colorful lettering on their end of the building announced S&C INVESTIGATIVE SERVICES with a phone number listed below the text. There were three empty parking spaces. Taking the one nearest the entrance, I parked and went in. The office was nicely decorated, Ikea modern, with some plants and a receptionist desk. Two smaller offices, along with a restroom and storage area, were at the back.

"Chloe, it looks like you are in business," I said to Chloe, who was still making final decorative changes.

"Sarah told me to shoot you if you showed up, but yes, it is coming along quite nicely. Sarah is at Office Depot getting some supplies. She should be back anytime now." And with that pronouncement, Sarah pulled into the second of the three spaces.

"Sean, I was anticipating your visit. Actually, I was expecting your curiosity to get the better of you earlier in the day. Well, what do you think?"

"It looks like you're in business, and, as you said, this is a great location, visible from Route 1. If you are ready to lock up for the day, let me take you lady sleuths out to dinner."

***

Three weeks later, Sarah is lamenting over our Friday night bottle of wine, "We haven't had a single customer. A couple from New

6

Hampshire stopped in last week asking for directions to Mount Vernon. Chloe wanted to charge them for the information ... but didn't."

"Give it time. Mark had a slow start, and that was with Wanda's referrals. It's also been slow at Eyeball. I think everyone is on vacation."

I got a call from Sarah on Tuesday, the tone somewhere between excited and despairing. "Sean, we had our first case today– a missing dog. A retired woman who lives three blocks from me had her 'puppy' go missing. Ralphie, a fifteen-year-old bulldog, is blind in one eye and partially deaf. We found him hiding in the bushes in a local park. Some young kids were terrorizing the poor dog. We retrieved Ralphie and returned him to the grateful widow. Chloe didn't want to take her money until I explained that Ralphie meant a great deal to the lady and that refusing payment would insult her. So, we made a few dollars, our first paying case."

Three days later, they got their second case. A missing eight-year-old boy. The mother, an illegal immigrant, was reluctant to go to the police fearing the family would be deported. The family being her husband, a day laborer, and two older daughters, the oldest working as a domestic and the other in high school.

Gonzales was playing with his friends Thursday afternoon and failed to show up for dinner. Maria, the middle sibling, was supposed to be watching him but was distracted by her boyfriend. The family and family friends searched for him late into the evening. Paulino, one of Gonzales's playmates, said he last saw Gonzales talking with a man standing beside a big black car. He ran away when the man tried to talk to him.

7

Time was critical. Sarah called one of her old partners at the FBI. Jessica was now working with the child abduction unit. After conveying the information Camila, the boy's mother provided the agent said, "I wish they had reported this kidnapping yesterday; the kidnapper has a twelve-hour head start. Sarah, I need you to talk with the mother. Tell her we are not going to deport them but need to know how they got into the country. Did a cartel bring them in? Does the cartel think the family still owes them money? Was the boy taken as a hostage to get payment? You need to have a heart-to-heart talk with the mother and father. They will probably be reluctant, fearing retaliation against the family. I'll call you later; in the meantime, I'll see what my informants have heard."

Chloe and Sarah go to the address Camila provided. It's an apartment complex, a cluster of four buildings, each a three-floor walkup. The tenants appear to be mostly Hispanic families, probably from Central America. They find Camila and her husband in their second floor, two-bedroom apartment. The parents have one bedroom, the two girls the second, and Gonzales has a small rollaway bed in the living room. It's a cramped apartment.

"Camila," Sarah starts, "is this your husband?"

"Yes, Miguel Morales."

"Okay, Camila, Miguel, I've contacted an old friend at the FBI. Don't look so horrified; you won't be deported. She works in the FBI's child abduction unit. She's started the process of looking for your son. She has some questions for you. Your answers will help us find Gonzales."

"Was a cartel involved in getting you into the US?"

After some hesitancy, Miguel answers, "Yes, the Sinaloa Cartel."

"Do you still owe them money or other favors?"

Again, after some delay and side glances at his wife, he answered, "Yes. They charged us ten thousand dollars. I pay a little every week, but they want more. Once, one of them said the entire debt could go away if we gave them Gonzales. I think they want to sell him."

"And can you provide any names?"

This time there was a long delay, with the couple forcing back tears of fear. Camila finally answers in a whisper, "Diego. He's the boss. The only other name I have is Alejandro. He is always with Diego. They will kill us if they find out we named them."

"Can you contact them?" Chloe asks.

"No," says Camila. "When they want us, they show up at the *abacería*, what you call the grocery store, or on the street.

"Do they have a car?" Sarah asks.

"Sometimes Diego is driving a loud red car. It looks new. Other times a third man is with them, driving an old black pickup truck."

"Anything else you can tell us?" asks Sarah.

"No," they both reply.

Okay, we are working on this. Call us if the kidnappers contact you or if you remember anything else."

3 Breakthrough

As the two enter their new office, Sarah is saying, "We will need the Bureau's resources on this. I'll call Jessica back with what we have. Mabey you can do a quick internet search on cartel activities in Northern Virginia."

"Jessica, this is Sarah. We talked with the Morales. The Sinaloa Cartel smuggled them into the country. They still owe the cartel over eight thousand dollars. The two names they have are Diego and Alejandro, but no contact information ... yes, they have had face-to-face meetings and can probably identify them."

Jessica asks, "Will they come into DC and talk with me?"

"I doubt it; they are scared shitless. They think the cartel is having them watched and are hunkered down protecting the two daughters."

"Jessica, I'm retired from the Bureau but still have some standing. Can you arrange for me to tap into the rogues' gallery of known cartel members to see if I can get a positive identification?"

"Okay, I'll work on that and text you a link. In the meantime, I'm going to contact Quantico. I understand they are working on a special project involving child trafficking."

Sarah turns to Chloe, "I should be getting access to the Bureau's database of cartel goons. Once we get their pictures, we can make another run at Gonzales's parents to see if we can get a positive identification. AND ... to make this more interesting, Quantico is working a special project on child trafficking."

Early the next morning, Sarah's cell chirps; she has a text from Jessica providing the URL for a secure FBI site. Using her cell, she goes to that URL and opens the FBI rogues' gallery of known cartel members.

"Okay, time to visit the parents again," she says and calls them to arrange a meeting.

"They are still afraid they are being watched. They'll meet us at the Shirlington Library in Arlington. Twelve thirty."

Chloe and Sarah find the parents in the back sitting area. Sarah talks with the librarian and obtains the use of one of the small meeting rooms. Now out of sight, the first thing Miguel says is that Diego called as they were leaving the apartment to tell him he had twenty-four hours to make good on his payment, the entire amount, or his son would be sold to an out-of-state buyer. The parents are in a state of near collapse. Sarah has her phone out and has Camila and Miguel slowly going through the thousands of pictures in the FBI's gallery. After forty minutes, Miguel identified one who he thinks is 'Diego.' Chloe pulls up his details on her laptop. Diego is, in fact, named Diego and is a known cartel member from San Salvador. He's wanted for a series of minor crimes and for possible ties to child trafficking. And was last seen in Montgomery County, Maryland.

After a few more minutes of searching, they identify Alejandro. He's identified as a cartel runner wanted for minor crimes.

11

Chloe asks for Miguel's phone. Looking at the recent call history, she finds Deigo's call. The calling number is blocked, but Chloe has a few tricks up her sleeve. She links the phone to her laptop and activates an application she developed at Eyeball. A proprietary applicant, probably, but it's on her computer. After a moment, she has Diego's number and the location from where the call was made.

Time is critical if they are to catch Diego if he's still at that location, an apartment complex in Falls Church.

Sarah calls Jennifer and asks that Lucinda be patched in. After some words back and forth as to why, Lucinda is soon on the line. Brushing initial pleasantries aside, Sarah brings Lucinda up to date, finishing by telling her the location Chloe has found and the need for speed.

Lucinda agrees but must first get her boss's approval before dispatching a team.

"Henry is assigned to your project, isn't he?" Sarah explodes, saying, "Call Sean and get the Eyeball team to that site! Time is critical."

"Henry and I are on our way. I'll call Sean for backup."

It's twenty-five miles from Quantico to Falls Church, in midday traffic that's about an hour. Forty minutes later, Lucinda wheels her Dodge Charger into the Seven Corners apartment complex that Chloe identified. Where to look? There are multiple apartment units here. All they have to go on are the mug shots of Diago and Alejandro. Lucinda and Henry take up watch by the large parking lot on the south side, Sarah and Chloe on the north. Twenty minutes later, Sean and Butch join the stakeout. The six pair of eyes have the block of apartments encircled.

12

Ten minutes after Eyeball's team's arrival and all phones linked, "I think I see Alejandro," Henry says. "He's just coming out of the building in the southeast corner. Looks like he's headed to that green pickup truck."

"I got him," says Butch as the team converges.

Lucinda, the only one with legal status, whips out her credentials and lights into him. "Where is the kid!!"

"Alejandro, you are under arrest for kidnapping. You might make it easier for yourself if you give up Diago.

"Not much chance of the happening," says Sean as he slams Alejandro up against the hood of the truck. A quick body search turns up an apartment key. Apartment 2-22B.

Sean and Lucinda are off, running to Bldg. 2, looking for apartment 22B. It's on the second floor. Knocking on the door, they get no response. Sean looks at Lucinda, "Imminent danger?"

"Yes," she answers, "break it open."

Sean's shoulder soon has the door open. Inside is a pigsty: pizza boxes, half-empty Chinese carryout cartons, dirty bedding, etc., but no sign of Gonzales.

An old man from the adjacent unit is standing at the door. The loudmouth left with the boy two hours ago. Lucinda shows him a photo of Diago, and he confirms the man is Diago. "He's driving a late model Camaro, red," the man says.

Lucinda calls the Arlington Police, identifies herself, and requests an Amber Alert be issued. She provides a description of the car, the driver with his photo and rap sheet, and the abducted 8-yr old boy's photo. Within minutes the alert is issued throughout Northern

13

Virginia, the District of Columbia, and adjacent Maryland counties. It is soon passed on to all law enforcement agencies in a five-hundred-mile radius.

Returning to where Butch is holding Alejandro, Lucinda starts her questioning. "Where is Diego taking the boy?"

With a smirk, Alejandro says, "What's it to you bitch!"

Lucinda asks her team to spread out to see if there are any witnesses.

"Now that we are alone, one more time, where is Diego?"

"F... you!"

Lucinda grabs a pressure point on Alejandro's trapezius muscle and squeezes. He drops to his knees in pain. She increases the pressure as he starts screaming. "Now we can try the other shoulder, or you can answer my question," she says.

"Breezewood, he's taking the kid to Breezewood to be picked up by the buyer," Alejandro says between gasps.

"We heard you on the other side of the complex," Sarah said.

4 Breezewood

One of the largest interstate truck rest areas on the East Coast is located in Breezewood. It's located just off the Pennsylvania Turnpike. Route 30 bisects two of its major truck servicing centers: The Flying J Mega Travel Plaza and The TA Travel Center. The western end of I-70 terminates here at the entrance to the latter. There are also several restaurants and motels. Many places where Gonzales can be handed over to his new 'owner.'

"Sean, how far is Breezewood from here?" Lucinda asks.

"It's about a hundred miles as the crow flies; make it a hundred fifty on the road. About a three-hour drive if you don't want to attract attention."

Lucinda calls the Arlington Police to update them on the kidnapper's probable destination. Unfortunately, she catches them just as the shifts are changing, and there is a thirty-minute delay in getting the updated information to the Maryland and Pennsylvania State Police.

Diego now has close to a three-hour head start.

Diego pulls into the Gateway Travel Plaza's side parking lot which is somewhat screened by landscaping trees. The buyer is there, waiting for them. He's driving a nondescript blue passenger van with three rows of seats and heavily tinted windows.

Getting out of his car Diego asks, "You got the money?"

The driver hands Diego a manila envelope which Diego dumps onto the hood of his car. There are eight bundles of 'franklins.' "Eight thousand as we agreed," says the van driver.

Diego puts the money back in the envelope. He tosses it into his car onto the passenger's seat as he pulls Gonzales from the backseat. Gonzales's hands are secured with duct tape. As he hands him over to the van driver, the driver says, "We need two more. One of our boys died last week, and one escaped."

"And that's not going to come back on you?" Diego mutters, concerned about it coming back on him.

"Not to worry. The local children's rescue group is on our payroll."

"Someone will call you next week. We may need to pick two kids up at the border. I don't think we have any more locally," Diego says as he gets back in his car.

He heads back to Maryland on I-70.

Just outside of Hancock, the Maryland State Police see a red Camaro traveling well in excess of the 70 MPH speed limit. Pulling it over, the trooper looks at the BOLO for a red Camaro with a Hispanic driver. The attached photo looks like the driver. He approaches the driver with his hand on his sidearm. As he starts to ask for Diego's license and registration, Diego fires a round from the Glock hidden in his jacket, hitting the trooper in his lower abdomen.

16

As the Camaro bursts out onto the road, the trooper from the ground empties his service weapon into the back of the fleeing car. One round hits Diego in his shoulder, next to the spine. Diego loses control of his car. It crashes through the guard rails and rolls down the embankment. Another of the trooper's shots had hit the gas tank. Gas was spilling over the crash site; it ignited.

The Maryland State Police contacted the FBI about the stop and resultant accident; word quickly filters back to Lucinda. It's only been fifteen minutes since they left the apartment complex, and she is just delivering Alejandro to the federal lockup in Alexandria.

"Henry, call Sarah and tell them we'll meet them at their office in fifteen minutes."

The three parking spaces in front of S&C INVESTIGATIVE SERVICES are full; the excess cars are taking up the adjacent business's allotted spaces.

Lucinda brings them up to date as to why they won't be questioning Diego. "The Maryland State Police troop intercepted Diego as he was returning. The trooper was shot; his vest saved him," Lucinda said. The trooper fired on the car as it sped away, hitting the car and causing the driver to lose control. The car was a fireball as it came to rest at the bottom of the embankment."

"It's our best guess Gonzales was delivered to the cartel's buyer at Breezewood," Lucinda starts. "We have no idea who the buyer is or where he went from there."

"Lucinda," Chloe asks, "can you get me copies of all the outside security tapes in that complex?"

17

"That will be over a hundred cameras. Yes. I'll get the local authorities to collect the tapes today, and we can start screening them tomorrow morning at Quantico. Just like old times," Lucinda says with a smile.

When Chloe gets to the FBI lab, Lucinda has three monitors set up. She has left Henry in charge of reviewing the tapes. He is at the first monitor and is viewing his second tape. Chloe takes the second station and Sarah the third. By mid-morning, they are all blurry-eyed. "Time for a break," Henry says.

"How many more tapes," Sarah asks.

Henry looks at the box the Pennsylvania State Police delivered, "Looks like we have about sixty more. We should be able to finish it today."

Sarah fires up her monitor after the break and loads the tape from the Gateway Travel Plaza. She fast forward it to the time span they've been screening, noon to three. Five minutes into the tape she sees a red Camaro pulling into the parking lot, driven by Diego. It pulls around to the left side of the building. Sarah locates the tape for that side of the building, fast forward it to the time matching the car's arrival, and there it is, pulling in beside an old dark blue passenger van, Ohio plate number AKJ-4928.

"I got it," she yells.

Henry and Chloe gather around. "Can you close in on the driver's face?" Cloe asks.

After some fiddling with the controls, Sarah captures a moderately good image of the driver.

"Pull that image, and let's see if he is in the FBI's database."

18

Henry calls Lucinda in; they need her password to access the database.

In short order, they have a match, Harold Griffin, age 47, and a long rap sheet of petty crimes.

Chloe is plunking away at her keyboard. She has tapped into the Ohio Department of Motor Vehicles. She yells, "The van is registered to JC Industries in Graysville, Ohio."

A few more minutes and a search of the state's business database has Chloe reporting that "JC Industries was established twenty-five years ago and makes special order tourist trinkets. The owner is Billy Cordell."

Henry pipes up, "Lucinda, time for a field trip? Eyeball is looking for some work. Should we pull in Sean and Butch?"

"You guys are under contract. Call Anderson, and let's get mobilized."

Things move rapidly after Henry calls. Anderson calls Sean into his office. "You were wondering what Henry was up to. Your escapade yesterday has resulted in you and Butch being drafted by Lucinda for a little field work. Pack your bag; you two are going to Ohio … today."

5 JC Industries

Lucinda has a helicopter waiting for them at Quantico, them being Lucinda, Sean, and his two rottweilers, Hery and Butch. Sarah and Chloe remain behind over their objections. They are needed to get the latest satellite data on the JC Industries' facilities, number of employees, and any other data they can think of, a role that Chloe is familiar with but new to Sarah; she is use to being at the pointy end of the spear.

Agents from the Parkersburg, West Virginia field office meet them with three black SUVs when they touch down and five local agents to provide support.

The coordinates Chloe provides places JC Industries twenty-five miles northeast of Parkersburg, just off OH State Road 26. From the satellite photos, there are three buildings, one that looks to be an old farmhouse. As they drive north, Sean and Lucinda are formulating their takedown plan.

"This smaller building must be where the kids are being kept,' Sean says. "If you look closely, you can see bars on the windows. The larger building is probably the workshop. It has a loading dock and driveway going up to it. The farmhouse is where we will find Billy and his crew."

"Okay, and then?" Lucinda asks.

"I suggest three agents take the workshop. You, Henry, and the remaining agents take the farmhouse entering it from these two points. Butch and I will tackle the smaller building. We can wait down the road here," I say, pointing to the map, "executing the plan at midnight. There is a full moon tonight, so we don't need lights approaching the targets."

The takedown goes off almost as planned if one discounts the fact that Billy had enough time to call his friend, the local police chief, to report a home invasion.

As Lucinda and the agents are securing the site, Butch and I are at the small building when two local police units pull up, lights flashing, sirens blaring, and guns drawn. As they make some feeble attempt to arrest Butch and me, I point them to the small building and ask if they condone child slave labor. Inside are five children, ages eight to twelve, chained to their beds, surplus army cots. It soon becomes evident that Billy has paid the cops off.

"Gentlemen," I say to the three officers, "let's put your guns on the ground and line up against the building; I think you are about to be arrested."

The police chief, a man that's fifty pounds overweight and with a flushed face, is laughing at me when Lucinda, with three heavily armed agents, materializes out of the trees and yells, "Now!"

I go into the room with the kids. I find Gonzales and tell him his parents are waiting for him. "Where are the keys for these handcuffs," I ask.

"The old man that runs this place has them."

Leaving Butch with the kids, I find Billy. "Billy, where are the keys?"

It appears he is reluctant to answer. A punch to his gut doubled him over. I grabbed a handful of his hair, lifting his face back up. "Keys!"

Gasping, he says, "Kitchen table."

I found the keys, and in short order, had all the kids unshackled.

Lucinda has the children taken to a local hospital to be checked over. In the morning, the questioning begins to determine who they are and can the authorities find parents or relatives.

The two younger children spoke only Spanish and could provide no useful identifying information. The two old kids said they last saw their family in Mexico. The coyote leading the group took the kids over the border separately, saying it was safer. Once in DHS facilities, one was given to a man claiming to be a relative. The other had a similar story. Gonzales was the only child that could be reunited with his parents.

Questioning Billy and Harold, the latter was found hiding in the farmhouse's root cellar, provided a little history of JC Industries. The business, started a quarter century ago by Billy's father, makes small novelty items for business promotions, knickknacks for local fairs, and items young children like to buy at travel centers on family road trips.

Junk from China was undermining the business. Five years ago, it was suggested to Billy that cartels could provide cheap labor. He took them up on it, contracting to buy five 'employees.'

As a child got too old, becoming a physical threat to Billy and Harold, the cartel would provide a replacement and dispose of the problem. The cartel charged a replacement transaction cost of between five and ten thousand dollars based on the circumstances.

***

Sarah is holding Gonzales's hand as she and the FBI agent walk him up the steps to his family's apartment. His mother is on her knees, hugging him. The father, teary-eyed, is shaking Sarah's hand, trying to pay her.

"The FBI did all the work. The retainer you gave us is all we need; we're good," Sarah tells Miguel.

That evening as Sarah and I are comparing notes, she says, "These people are evil. I've asked Lucinda to use Chloe and me, at no cost, if we can help save other kids."

5 Freddy

Over the next few months, Sarah and Chloe are retained by the FBI under the Eyeball contract to assist Lucinda in the 'Stolen Youth' program.

At the monthly FBI Department Head meeting, the Crime Division Head, Agent Wainwright, reports on Lucinda's recent successes. Later as he's leaving the Hoover Building, I intercept him. "Jacob, you have time for lunch?"

"Sean, yes, but no lobbying for Sarah's company. She is doing quite well without you."

"I know. You always think I want something when I invite you to lunch?"

"Let's go to Sampson's grill, and you can surprise me," Jacob says.

After we are seated and lunch is ordered, I start, "Anderson and I will be out-of-pocket for the next several weeks. We are undertaking one of his special projects ... in Europe this time. Adam will be in charge at Eyeball."

"A secret mission for the CIA?" Jacob says with a wink.

"No, a private undertaking. If you're good, I may tell you about it someday."

Earlier that week

"Do you remember Major Freedman?" Anderson asks one morning as we both arrive at work. Spending a few minutes in the parking lot, Anderson brings me up to speed on his latest project.

"Freddy, yes. He was our contact in the British Virgin Islands which led to us recovering the Nazi gold. What does he have to do with it?"

"You may recall he claimed some knowledge of the sunken sub long before we got involved. His story is that in 1945 one of the crew members slipped away from the beached sailors in French Guyana and made his way north to Paramaribo, the capital city of Suriname, as the others went south to Brazil."

Freddy's father was with the British Diplomatic Corps in the late '40s, assigned to consular duties in British Guyana. One of the family's household staff had relatives in Paramaribo. To make a long story short, Freddy came into possession of the briefcase the sailor took from the sub. In it is what he believes is Joseph Goebbels's diary. Major Freedman is getting along in years and decided it was time to do something with it. Three months ago, he contacted me … proposing a partnership."

"Partnership, to publish a diary?"

"I've sent Adam down there to assess the credibility of Freddy's claim," said Anderson. "He called last week to report, from what he can tell, the diary looks to be authentic. Chloe, before her departure,

25

was working with him to compare the handwriting in the diary with known samples of Goebbels's scribble. They match."

"I've tasked Adam to negotiate a partnership agreement with Freddy. Our retained legal staff, Begley, Bedlam, and Booze, are working with Adam."

As we drift into the reception area, I see a familiar face, Major Freedman.

Seeing us, he gets up to meet us. "Bill, you're looking good for your age, and who is this youngster with you," says a grinning Freddy.

"Cut the BS Freddy; the bar's not open yet," responds Anderson. "let's find some coffee, and then the three of us can discuss your diary."

Seated in his office, coffee in hand, Anderson turns to me, "I'm sure you've heard the urban legend about 'Hitler's Treasure Train' when you were stationed in Germany, a train laden with gold and art treasures that were hidden by the Nazis in southwest Poland during the last days of World War II. Historians believe the train never existed."

"Goebbels's diary claims otherwise. I'm thinking of going to Germany to look for it," says an enthusiastic Anderson.

"A boondoggle to Europe based on a dead Nazi's ramblings," I quip. "What's the prize, stolen art? Secret documents? Hitler's lost love nest?" I say tongue-in-cheek.

"And if this doesn't work out, we can turn this into a boondoggle," said Anderson. "I'm due a vacation, and this will give me a chance to visit my German son,"

Before giving the diary to Anderson, Freddy says, "I want 10 percent of the gross proceeds Eyeball realizes, and I retain publication rights to the diary. I also want to go with you and be part of the discovery team."

"Yes, yes, and no," says Anderson. "You'd have us stopping at every other gästehaus to sample their brew, and more to the point, you have several years on me and will slow us down."

"Freddy, you've read the agreement our lawyers have drawn up, and I assume your people have reviewed it. Let's get it signed, and I can start the wheels turning."

After they both sign the agreement and he has the diary in hand, Anderson offers my services to drive Freddy to National Airport, where he's scheduled on a flight back to the Islands.

Anderson calls Caroline into his office. "Caroline here is your first major project. I'm sure recent office scuttlebutt has focused on Goebbels's diary. Here it is. Your first task is to digitize it and return it to me, along with a digitized version on a thumb drive. A second digital copy is to be kept by you. Do not load it into the Eyeball database, and don't share it.

"Your second task is to find out all you can about the treasure train."

With the wheels turning, Anderson bids Freddy a safe trip home and a promise to keep him in the loop.

Freddy and I get to experience the tail-end of DC rush hour traffic, and I-95 does not disappoint. It takes over an hour for us to get north of Quantico, normally a thirty-minute drive.

"I heard your significant other has set up a business for herself. A lovely lady. I enjoyed showing you two around the island when you visited." Freddy is referring to our Virgin Islands vacation, one that Sarah keeps suggesting we repeat.

"Your flight is not until four; let's stop and pick Sarah up for lunch," I say. "She'll enjoy seeing you again."

"S&C INVESTIGATIVE SERVICES, impressive," Freddy says. Sarah is surprised to see Freddy, and Chloe has questions about the history of the diary. The two quickly agreed to join us for lunch.

6 Treasure Train

The following day Caroline reports back to Anderson,

"According to the legend, in the last months of World War II, a Wehrmacht train, nicknamed '*Der Goldener Zug*,' laden with treasures plundered from eastern Europe left Breslau, now Wrocław, Poland passed through Schlesien, and disappeared. The train was suspected to have entered an abandoned coal mine or tunnel system, which was then part of the unfinished, top-secret Nazi construction site in Poland. Onboard the train was rumored to be more than three hundred thirty tons of gold, jewels, and artistic masterpieces. This is a popular legend," said Caroline.

Caroline continues, "Goebbels's diary has an interesting reference to the Lusatian Mountain range in the southeast corner of the old East Germany. Goebbels claims in his diary that the train bypassed Waldenburg, today known as Wałbrzych, and was diverted south to Liberec in the Sudetenland, with its final destination being the Görlitz district of Saxony, where Goebbels had it buried in a subterranean munition production facility."

"In the last years of WWII, Germany moved critical manufacturing facilities underground, into old mines, newly created bunkers, anywhere to get them away from Allied air raids," said Caroline. "The Lusatian Mountains are laced with spent coal mines that were abandoned in the early 1900s."

"Research into Germany's war production efforts in the later years of the war makes mention of a small arms munitions facility near Zittau, the southeasternmost city in Saxony," said Caroline. The exact location is now unknown. The Nazis had all evidence of rail lines going into the mountains removed by slave labor, who were all conveniently disappeared by May 1945."

Anderson calls me and Adam into his office and has Caroline repeat her findings. "I think we have a plausible scenario," Anderson says. "Thoughts?"

"Weren't the East German authorities ever curious about the train legend? They controlled this area for forty years. They were the recipients of local records, Nazi records." Adam comments.

"Apparently, Goebbels laid such a base of lies and false leads pointing to Poland that there was never any serious consideration that the train ever intended to go to Saxony," responded the Colonel.

"And we believe his diary?"

"Yes. Sean, here is the name of my contact at the army archives in Kansas, General DeWitt. They have warehouses full of captured WWII documents. Contact him and see if there are any pre-1940 Wehrmacht maps of the area. You may have to offer to assist in the search."

Oh great, another trip to the hinterlands, I'm thinking.

"Adam, if you would, see what you can find out about today's conditions in Saxony?"

I had some surprising success in Kansas. The Germans are meticulous record keepers. Not only did I find the requested Wehrmacht map, but I also found the German Automobile Club *(Allgemeiner Deutscher Automobil)* maps from the late '30s and topographical maps prepared by the German Geological Society.

"General DeWitt was very helpful," I tell Anderson, "he sends his regards. The older maps I found show a rail line connecting Zittau and Liberec; those lines are still shown on today's maps. What is missing from today's maps is the feeder line going into the Lusatian Mountains, about a fifteen-mile stretch of track passing through Jonsdorf."

Adam jumps in at this point, saying, "Most of this area is now a nature preserve, the Zittau Mountain Nature Park. It's a popular destination for weekend trekkers. Any excavation will be met with great resistance. The Germans have a mythical attachment to their forests."

7 The Ex

A few weeks later, Anderson's 'Goldener Zug' team is winging across the Atlantic, Colonel Anderson me. Eyeball has booked us on Lufthansa in business class. I'm in the aisle seat, Anderson beside me.

"Colonel, I'm curious, and please tell me to stuff it if I'm overstepping. Earlier, you mentioned visiting your German son. I didn't know you had a German family."

Anderson is about to tell me to stuff it but then thinks otherwise.

"Sean, we've been together for many years. I've kept my personal life private. Not many people know I am divorced, and my youngest son lives in Germany. In the early '70s, Margaret, my first wife, died in childbirth. The baby survived. Johnathan, whom you have met, is now in his 50s, living in Falls Church along with my two grown grandchildren. Due to multiple overseas deployments, my older sister raised Johnathan accepting Johnathan into her brood of children, five if one is counting. I've maintained very close contact with him over the years and have a strong father-son relationship.

"In the mid-70s, I met Giselle, the daughter of a German automotive engineer, Earnest Zimmerman, who, at the time, was on the team opening a new VW plant in Georgia.

"I think you may have met her once while we were both stationed at Fort Benning."

"Yes. I vaguely remember you with a petite blond with an enchanting accent."

"That petite blond turned out to be a '*Deutsche Hexe.*' Shortly after our wedding vows, it became obvious that this union was not going to work. Giselle backtracked on her commitment to accept Johnathan as her stepson, and she soon resented my overseas deployments. She filed for divorce in the late '70s and moved back to her father's estate in Stuttgart. It wasn't until two years later that I learned of my second son. Rudolph was born in Germany. Under German family law, a non-German living in another country, divorced, and the child born in Germany had no parenting rights. Giselle shut me out of his early life."

"I've made an attempt to get to know him. He is now in his late thirties, an established lawyer working at Kirkland & Ellis International in Munich. Over the years, I visited him at school and later in Munich as he started his professional life. During my last visit, he invited me to meet my new granddaughter."

"And Giselle?"

"A bitter old lady, living by herself on a large estate," the Colonel said.

8 Jonsdorf

We fly into Frankfort and catch a connecting flight to Dresden, the capital city of the German state of Saxony. The city was spared Allied air attacks until the final days of WWII ... when the Allied fire-bombed the city. Buildings not bombed, burned. Rather than repair them, the East German authorities razed the ruins of many churches, royal buildings, and palaces in the '50s and '60s, as well as many historic residential buildings. The surroundings of the once lively Prager Strasse resembled a wasteland before it was rebuilt in the socialist style. But there were also many historic buildings saved or reconstructed. Today Dresden is one of the most visited cities in Germany with a thriving economy.

Anderson's secretary made reservations for us at a small hotel overlooking the Elbe River in the *Äußere Neustadt* district, the part of Dresden located outside the old city walls. Today the area is known for its thriving bars and clubs.

We were in the air for eight hours and six hours into the next day due to time changes. In other words, it was midafternoon the following day from when we left. Anderson's travel theory was to 'power' through time changes and retire at his usual time in the new time zone. The theory is to quickly get your body clock back in sync with the local time. I subscribe to this theory; it works.

We checked in and agreed to meet in twenty minutes in the reception area.

Stepping out of the hotel I ask, "What now?"

"It's early yet. I saw a park, a block that way, next to the river. Let's take a short walk, stretch our legs, and review our plan."

Walking along the riverside, I say, "The plan, that's simple. We drive to Jonsdorf tomorrow, find a place to stay and then look around without attracting attention. We have the old maps. We see if we can find the old rail bed. Follow it to its end, find a cave, and inside is the *Goldener Zug*. What am I missing?"

Anderson looks at me and shakes his head. "There's a restaurant over there. Let's get something to eat, and then I'm going to get a good night's sleep while you're out partying."

"If I were only twenty years younger … but a good night's sleep is now hard to pass up."

***

We're on the road early the next morning. The countryside is mostly rolling hills with farmland in the valleys. In a little less than two hours, we are in Jonsdorf, in the Lusatian Mountains.

Jonsdorf dates back to the sixteenth century when it was established as a sandstone quarry to produce millstones. Today it is a small village nestled in the Lusatian Mountains, catering to weekend hikers visiting the nature park.

I see a café with what appears to be a shared space with a bakery. "Time for a coffee break," I tell Anderson, "and maybe some pastries."

We claim one of the sidewalk tables and a middle-aged lady dressed in regional finery comes to take our order.

"That's a fancy serving outfit you have on," Anderson says in fluent German.

"The boss requires that we all be dressed in traditional costumes. He thinks it attracts tourists. Were you attracted?" she says with a sly smile.

"No, I was just tired of driving and wanted a short rest," I said in my broken German. "Coffee and fresh pastries are a bonus."

She laughs and takes our order. When she returns with her tray, Anderson asks, "We're here for a couple of nights. Can you recommend a place we can stay?"

"Romantik Hotel, just up the hill," she says, pointing.

As we're leaving, she catches Anderson's eye and says with a wink, "My name is Gertrude; I'm always here."

The hotel is picturesque, probably built in the nineteenth century. The desk is manned by an older man. His brisk nature does not recommend him for this job, and he appears indifferent as we get two rooms for two days.

Anderson is able to get a hiking guide from him showing the local trails into the mountains. "If you get lost," he says, "you are on your own. Nobody is going to come looking for you."

We drop our backpacks off in our room, and as we are leaving the hotel, a woman's voice calls out. "I must apologize for Carl. My

36

normal clerk is out sick today. I'm Frau Decker, owner of the Romantik Hotel. Carl is my deceased husband's older brother. As you can probably tell, he's not a people person. He normally tends to the hotel's maintenance. If there is anything you need, please let me know."

We are dressed in jeans, hiking boots, and flannel shirts. Two old men out for a hike in the mountain. Using the map Anderson coerced out of Carl, we find the nearest trailhead. The trailhead is not far from the site of the now nonexistent rail line as shown on our pre-WWII maps. We headed up the trail looking for hints of an old mine.

"It's been close to eighty years since Goebbels had the train hidden and tracks removed," said Anderson. "That's enough time for a mature forest to grow and eradicate most natural landmarks."

The mountainside south of Jonsdorf is laced with hiking trails and shares the border with the Czech Republic, a half mile south. We spend the better part of the day exploring the area where we think the nineteenth century coal mine was located. On one side of a ridge, we find a depressed area that is somewhat straight and in alignment with the general area of the car park. It extends for about a mile taking it across the border. Is this the collapsed cave?

9 Carl

That evening Anderson and I had a delicious dinner served by Frau Decker in the hotel's dining room. Anderson invites her to sit with us and tell us about the hotel's history. She readily accepts.

"The Romantik Hotel has been in my husband's family since the early 1800s, much like you see it today. In WWII, it catered to Nazi officials from Berlin. My father-in-law was working for them, but I didn't know what he was doing. I think it involved the removal of the train line from Zittau in the spring of 1945. Local rumors hint of a massive treasure hidden in the hills. The old Bürgermeister and other city officials laugh at this rumor. They claim the Nazi officials were simply on an inspection tour. As for the rail track, they said steel was needed for the war effort."

"Carl is quite a bit older than me. He was close to his father and probably knows more. You can find him at the Gasthaus Zum Lindengarten next door. He may still be coherent," Frau Decker mumbles the last part under her breath.

As predicted, we find Carl, with a stein of beer in hand, talking with some friends. We find a vacant table and order two steins of the local brew. It's actually quite good.

We waited for an opportune time to approach Carl. When his two friends get up to leave, it's time to strike. We order him another stein and ask the barmaid to point us out to him. She does, and Carl is soon sitting at the table with us.

"You didn't get lost I see," says Carl.

"No, the trails are well marked," said Anderson.

Carl asks why we are in Jonsdorf. "We get many German tourists, some from other countries, but few Americans."

"We are NATO consultants working in Poland with the redeployed American forces based in Wrocław," I answer. "We were just looking for a break from the monotony, and Jonsdorf looked like an interesting point on the map. I'm a history buff; I like the stories small towns like Jonsdorf have."

Carl looks at me and smiles. With a somewhat slurred voice, he goes on, "My family has been here for centuries. My great-great-great grandfather owned one of the first sandstone mines. His mill wheels were famous. Later my family brought coal mining to Jonsdorf. That lasted until the start of the last century when the mines were no longer profitable. We closed them down. The weekend tourist trade was developing prior to the Great War, and then everything went to shit. The *frosch* kept their boots on our necks, and then the Jews created a depression. Hitler restored our dignity."

"Many Nazi bigwigs visited Jonsdorf during the war," I said, "and they had the rail line removed; steel for the war effort?"

"My father hosted some of the biggest names in the Party. We donated the rail line for the effort. Nicky's Barn is all that remains."

"Nicky's barn?"

39

"Over by the new '*parkplatz*' at the base of the mountain," Carl slurs.

Two burly locals come looking for Carl. Seeing him, they come to our table, "Frau Decker sent us to collect Carl. After a few beers he tends to ramble on about a fanciful past," they explain. "Please excuse him."

After Carl is escorted out, I turn to Anderson, "Nicky's Barn? I think we need to investigate."

***

The following morning, we decided to get coffee at the café we first visited and pump Gertrude for local information. She is there as promised, warmly greeting Anderson as we take the table we had yesterday.

After we are served, Gertrude remains by our table. "Gertrude," Anderson starts, "my friend here is into local histories of small villages. Do you have any interesting stories about Jonsdorf?"

She thinks for a minute, "No. I've lived here all my life. Nothing exciting ever happens. Now my mother, may she rest in peace, had stories from when she was a girl. The comings and goings of Party officials. She claims to have seen Herr Goebbels. One night the army brought a train in, in the middle of the night. A few days later inmates from a camp in Poland were brought in to remove the train tracks. All very strange."

"What is Nicky's Barn?" I ask.

"Oh, that. It's a barn for Herr Nicholas's dairy cows. It's over by the *parkplatz*. You can't miss it. Now that could be an interesting story; there're rumors that local officials occasionally meet there."

As we are walking back to the hotel, Anderson asks, "Nicky's Barn, up for a little undercover investigation?"

We planned to leave the area today, driving through the Czech Republic on our way to Munich. Checking out of the Hotel, we thank Frau Decker for her hospitality. "We may be back in a few days," Anderson tells her. "My son is a workaholic. This would be a great place for him to unwind. All I have to do is convince him to take a few days off."

At the *parkplatz*, there is a pasture off to the right with a half dozen cows. On the far side of the pasture, there is a large barn, 'Nicky's Barn?'

We decided the best approach is to hike up the trail and then cut into the woods, approaching from the backside. As we get a closer view of the barn through the trees, we see it is built into the mountainside. As we were about to scale the fence, the two brawny lads that escorted Carl home last night burst from the barn making a beeline for us.

"Damn," curses Anderson, "we must have tripped a sensor."

The bigger of the two, somewhat aggressively, asks why we are climbing the fence.

"We got turned around in the woods and are trying to get back to the car park on the far side of the pasture," I say.

With skepticism, he says, "You could just follow the fence around."

"Yes, but it's a straight line from here to there," I snap back.

"Go back up the hill," he points, "about one hundred meters you will find the trail. Follow it downhill to the *parkplatz*."

As we drive away, Anderson says, "That was interesting."

10 Munich

Our trip to Munich through the Czech Republic is shorter than if we went via Dresden. We spent the night in Prague, a city that neither Anderson nor I have visited. It's a beautiful medieval city with many colorful baroque buildings. War damage was minor when compared with other European cities. The city's main claim to WWII fame is the assassination of Reinhard Heydrich in 1942 which occurred on a nearby country road and resulted in a brutal retribution by the SS.

It is only a couple hour drive from Prague to Munich. "What are our plans when we get there," I ask Anderson.

"I'm going to spend some time with my son; you are going to do some research. I want you to go to the *Zechenmuseum der Bundesrepublik Deutschland*. In English, that's the Coal Mine Museum of Germany. Caroline has been busy. She found a reference to this museum. She claims it has information on 'all' significant coal mines in Germany going back to the eighteenth century. Hopefully, there is information on the Jonsdorf mine. But first, I want you to meet Rudolph. He's arranged lunch for us."

Our destination is the Kirkland & Ellis International, LLP's building on Maximilian Strasse. We find a parking facility at the end of the street near the Isar River.

Rudolph is waiting for us in the lobby. Rudolph is a young man in his 40s, a spitting image of the Colonel I work for in my youth.

"Sean, this is Rudolph Zimmerman. Zimmerman is my ex's maiden name."

Rudolph turns to me, "My dad told me about some of your exploits; cartel drug smugglers and jihadis. Perhaps you can tell me more over a beer some night. And by the way, please call me Rudi."

"I've made lunch reservations for us at The Kaiser's Restaurant here in the business district. It's one of the few buildings not damaged in the war. The building dates back to the 1550s and is a beautiful example of baroque architecture."

Anderson and his son spend much of their time catching up; I sit and listen. I'm surprised when Anderson asks Rudolph what he knows about Hitler's *Goldener Zug*.

"It's a fairytale," says Rudolph.

"I don't think so. I think we," pointing to me, "know where it is." Anderson goes on to tell him much more than I'm comfortable with.

We had an excellent meal, and I told Rudolph it was nice meeting him. Later, on our way to our hotel, I said, "Don't you think you told him too much?"

"No, I want him involved in this, at least tangentially. I think he will be able to help. I'm going to spend the next couple of days with him. You have your tasking."

Over the next two days, I only see, passing is a better term, Anderson at the hotel's breakfast bar.

44

I found the *Zechenmuseum der Bundesrepublik Deutschland* on the city's outskirts. It is a private museum requiring an appointment to visit.

Herr Dumberg, the museum's curator, a wizened old man, welcomes me, "We don't have many visitors. How can I help you?"

"I'm looking for information on the Jonsdorf coal mine."

"Jonsdorf?" he repeats with a puzzled look.

"It is in the Görlitz district in Saxony."

"It must be a minor mine; I don't recognize the name ... but then there are many names I have forgotten over the years. Let me look in my files."

He goes to a large file cabinet with a hundred or more index card drawers. He fingers through two and, with the third drawer, exclaims, "Here it is. A small mine opened in 1852 in the Lusatian Mountains."

"Yes, that's it," I say. "What can you tell me about the mine."

"Well, let's see what we have in our files," says Herr Dumberg. I follow him into a small dusty room, "We don't come in here often," he says as he goes to an old file cabinet and pulls out a thin folder.

Reading the file, he says, "There appears to have been a long-standing dispute with the Austria-Hungarian empire about the mine intruding into their territory. The mine closed in 1901, no longer profitable. The dispute was never resolved. Oh, and here is a sketch of the mine showing the two, no three seams of coal. It looks like there were two entrances to the complex. The primary one appears to be in Jonsdorf, the other, over the border in Austria-Hungary, now the Czech Republic."

"This is most helpful," I say. "Can I get a copy of the file?"

45

With a sly smile, he says, "Copies are free to museum members. Otherwise, it will take me a week or more to get permission to make a copy, and the cost will be....."

Taking the hint, "And how much to become a museum member?"

"Five hundred euros, cash; the museum gets so little income these days," he says with a sigh.

"Sign me up," I say as I pull out my wallet.

11 Planning

On the third morning, Anderson is ready to talk. He comes and sits at my table with his bowl of cornflakes. "That's not much of a breakfast," I observed.

"Healthier than that plate of cholesterol you have. And thank you for asking; I had a good visit with Rudolph. He might be able to provide some help. And your endeavors, you found the coal mine museum?"

Okay, he's the boss, so I shared first. I told him I was now a proud dues-paying member of the *Zechenmuseum der Bundesrepublik Deutschland*. I related what I learned of the Jonsdorf mine.

"Other than the border conflict with Austria-Hungry, that's what we already knew. Not worth whatever your membership cost," he said in a dismissive tone.

"Well thank you for your support. You probably will also dismiss the map I have. As a dues-paying member of the museum, I obtained a map showing the location of the mine's three shafts, the smaller one crossing the border into the Czech Republic. Eyeball owes me five hundred euros. Not a shabby investment."

At this news, Anderson perks up, "Where is this map?"

"In my room; I wasn't expecting we'd be talking this morning."

He is now excited and asks me to get it. I leave my breakfast, giving it a longing glance as I leave for my room. My plate is cold by the time I return. Anderson offers to order a replacement. I wave him off as we start to discuss the map.

Using the Google app, he pulls up a map of the Jonsdorf area. "There are several small inns in the Czech Republic just across the border from Jonsdorf," he says. "A couple not far from the end of that smaller shaft where your map shows where there is or was an entrance to the mine. I wonder if it is still there?"

"That brings me to my information. Rudolph wants to work with us."

"Not a good idea," I say.

"Agreed, I told him no. He offered to provide legal assistance if needed. He could get the firm to provide a family discount rate.

"He also offered to contact an old college roommate who now works for the *Bundeskriminalamt*, the Federal Criminal Police Office, Germany's equivalent to our FBI. Again, I said no. But then on second thought, I asked him to keep his friend on speed dial in case we needed to engage the authorities."

"Okay," I said, "it sounds like it's time we explore the backdoor approach to Jonsdorf."

"One more thing I should tell you," said Anderson. "I called Adam last night asking if he would convince Henry and Lucinda to take a short German vacation. My gut is telling me we will need backup. I'll coordinate with him later today."

Over the years, experience has taught me to trust Anderson's gut.

12 Surprises

Anderson promised Rudolph we'd meet him for lunch before we left. Rudolph suggested a small café not far from his office. Rudolph was there when we arrived. He was not alone. A lady was sitting with him., a snow princess from Tchaikovsky's Waltz of the Snowflakes, blond hair and crystal blue eyes.

"Dad," he starts, "I'm sorry for asking Agent Hoffman to join us. I mentioned the treasure train to my boss. He didn't want details and thought the story was a myth, but if the story had legs, the State had to be involved. I contacted Gundula, the friend I mentioned earlier. As a favor to me, she agreed to meet with us."

Looking at Anderson, I could tell he was pissed. He covered it well though, saying, "Agent Hoffman, thank you for your interest. How much has Rudolph told you?

"He told me about Goebbels's diary and your recent visit to Jonsdorf. It all sounds iffy to me, but after someone found Goebbels's submarine, also an old rumor, I guess anything is possible."

Anderson considers what to say next. "Agent Hoffman, I can't say I'm happy you're here. It was not my choice, but it's done. You're involved."

"Please call me Gundi; this is all unofficial," she said.

"I think the treasure train is real and that we know where to find it. This man across the table from you," pointing at me, "is the one who found the sunken U-Boat. He helped the Argentine authorities dismantle a nest of Nazis and recovered five tons of gold." We had less to go on then than we do now. The gold train is real, and we're going to find it. If you don't interfere with our efforts, we will keep you involved. Do we have a deal?"

Looking at me, Gundi nods her agreement and says, "After this is over, you have to tell me about the submarine. It's rumored that the Mossad took all the gold."

She hands cards to Anderson and me. "He is my cell number; call me anytime. I can provide you backup if needed."

As we take our leave, Rudolph is saying, "Use her; she's discreet, well connected with senior officials in the *Bundeskriminalamt*, and is a decorated officer. As a bonus, she's a martial arts instructor at the police academy."

Driving out of the city, Anderson is still fuming, "I didn't want any outside help, at least not yet."

"Well, we got it, so let's put Gundi in our tool bag; she could be useful."

Shortly after crossing into the Czech Republic Anderson's cell rings. It's Andy. "Boss, I have Lucinda and Henry here. They're looking forward to a German vacation." Lucinda and Henry are an item who fill the role of a vacationing couple.

Lucinda starts, "Jacob begrudgingly gave me a two-week leave of absence from the Bureau; he felt he owed you. Henry and I will be

51

there tomorrow; we fly out of Dulles tonight. Where do you want us?"

Lucinda is an FBI cyber analyst and has worked with Eyeball personnel on numerous occasions. She is five foot eight, has red hair, and sports dragon tattoos reminiscent of her Viking heritage. Lucinda is lethal, having black belts in several martial art disciplines.

Her former boss, Agent Dillion, assassinated last year, was replaced by Jacob Wainwright as the new Crime Division Head, but that's another story. Dillion claimed she has a black belt in dirty fighting and that FBI martial art instructors would not spar with her.

Henry is a former Navy SEAL. Many years ago, Anderson assigned him, along with two others, as my protection detail when the North Koreans were after me. The trio became known as 'Sean's rottweilers.' He's been with me on several assignments, saving my ass more than once. He was with me in Argentina when we recovered the Nazi gold.

With these two having our backs, what could go wrong?

Anderson gives them directions to Jonsdorf. "Check into any hotel other than the Romantik Hotel. Try the Hotel Gondelfahrt," he says. "It overlooks where we think the old mine is located."

He goes on, "We are staying just over the border in the Czech Republic for now. I think Sean found a backdoor to the mine. I'll call you in two days."

I'm chuckling to myself; Anderson asks what's funny? "I'm just picturing Lucinda and Gundi working together," I answer.

13 Czech Republic

We find a small inn on the Czech Republic side of the Lusatian Mountain range. As the crow flies, it is only a few miles from Jonsdorf and not far from where we think the second entrance to the Jonsdorf mine is located.

We're up early. Our hostess is just laying out pastries and brewing coffee for the guests. There are two Japanese couples and a trio of English trekkers.

Frau Scholtz, our hostess in idle conversation, asks the group what their plans are for the day.

The Japanese are leaving for Prague after they checkout and our English trekkers say they are headed to Zawidów, a small town on the Polish and Czech Republic border.

"Thank god," whispers Anderson to me. "I was afraid they would interfere with our plans."

After my second *Berliner*, known back home as a jelly doughnut, Anderson pulls me away. Turning to Frau Scholtz says, "I think I saw a marker for trail just off the road. Where does it go? Up the mountainside?"

"Yes, it's a couple hour hike to the top. Would you like some sandwiches to take with you?

"Yes, thank you," says Anderson.

Anderson and I soon find ourselves deep in the forest following a poorly marked trail. At the base of what looks like a small cliff line, Anderson pulls out his GPS gizmo and asks to see my maps. Using the topological map, overlayed with my *Zechenmuseum* map showing the mine tunnels, Anderson points to the west saying, "The tunnel entrance should be about a mile in that direction."

We're off the trail now; the underbrush is thick. We follow the cliff line for several hundred yards. I'm the first to see it, an old shed that has barely survived the creeping undergrowth.

"Part of the mine operation?" Anderson wonders.

We kick a few boards aside, there is nothing inside. "Check the hillside," Anderson says.

After a few minutes fighting with the brambles, Anderson calls out, "I found something." Pulling back the bushes, Anderson sees a cave entrance secured by an old iron gate. The gate is overgrown with vines and well concealed from view.

Pulling the vines back, we find the hinges are rusted and what is left of a lock securing the gate. After a few good solid tugs, we had the gate open wide enough to let us slip in.

We both have tac lights. After the first fifty feet of rubble, the cave becomes a proper tunnel. At its lowest point, it is five feet high, and the narrowest is four feet. It's easygoing until we encounter significant rubble blocking our way. Anderson, peering over the top thinks he can see open space. We spent the next two hours moving

54

small boulders. Slowly the opening is wide enough for us to crawl through.

The tunnel bends gently to the right, and there it is … the back end of a boxcar. The space between the boxcar and the tunnel wall is hardly wide enough to allow passage. At more than one point we had to get on all fours and crawl beside the track under the boxcar. In total, there are four boxcars. There is no possibility of getting into one as long as they are in the tunnel; the tunnel walls and ceiling make it too snug.

There is a wooden wall constructed across the tunnel at the head of the line of boxcars with a small door. Anderson motions for me to open it.

The door opens, and we find ourselves in a well-appointed conference room. Our door is located behind a large banner, one of several Nazi banners in the room. On one wall is a large painting of Hitler. Beneath it is a large ledger listing the chapter members of the '*Loyale Bruderschaft*,' Loyal Brotherhood.

Carl is identified as the group's '*Erster Feldwebel*,' First Sargent. I point out Frau Decker's name to Anderson. She's listed as the '*Kommandant der Einheit*,' the Unit Commander.

Anderson, who has been taking photos on his iPhone, snaps several of the ledger.

At the far end of the conference room, there is another door, a more prominent door. We crack it open and are looking at the interior of a barn, a dairy barn. Pulling it shut, Anderson motions for us to leave. He saw one of the two men who had earlier escorted us off the property.

We make our way back the way we came. It is early evening by the time we are back at the inn.

"I'm so glad to see you!" said Frau Scholtz. "In another half hour, I was going to call the rescue crew. You don't know how many hikers get lost in these woods."

As I'm thanking Frau Scholtz for her concern Anderson is calling Henry. I heard the end of his call. "We'll meet you in Zittau for lunch tomorrow. Find a restaurant near the train station. We can coordinate the place and time later."

14 Captured

We have a little admin work to do that evening. We both uploaded all our information, the photos Anderson took, and my information on the Jonsdorf mine file, including a photo of the mine's map. After confirming successful uploads, we scrub our phones. We didn't want any of this information falling into the wrong hands if a phone is misplaced.

Anderson called Adam to get updates on some of Eyeball's current contracts. Butch, one of my three rottweilers, has been assigned to work with S&C INVESTIGATIVE SERVICES, now the FBIs lead contractor on its child trafficking investigation. They've had some success in climbing the cartel chain of command by identifying Diego's boss.

I called Emanual Castro, SIDE's Deputy Assistant for Internal Affairs. SIDE is the *Argentine Secretaría de Inteligencia*. I met Castro a couple of years ago when we recovered the Nazi gold and indirectly helped him break up the *Adler Bruderschaft*, the nest of Argentine Nazis headed by **Papa Dumberg**.

"Emanual, this is Sean. ... Yes, the Sean who made off with all the gold," I said as he started giving me a hard time about Mossad's role in our adventure.

"I need your help. I'm in Germany and have tripped over a Nazi cell that may have had contact with Nazi cells in South America. You impounded all of Papa Dumberg's papers. Did he name any contacts for like-minded cells in Germany? … Yes, you should have got a portion of the gold, but it all went to a good cause supporting holocaust survivors. If you can help me with this, Colonel Anderson would be grateful. If you find anything, please call Adam at Eyeball; you have the number, and he will get the information to me."

We are on the road by ten the next morning when Henry calls, telling us where to meet him and Lucinda.

Zittau is the southeasternmost city in the German state of Saxony. The city is a key transit point between the Czech Republic, Germany, and Poland. It is within ten miles of Jonsdorf, but with people coming and going, it is a good place to meet without being noticed, and near the train station, no one stands out.

Entering the restaurant, I spot Lucinda's red hair in a booth on the other side of the room. We join them, order lunch, and Anderson fills them in on all we've found.

"What's the plan?" Henry asks.

"Sean and I will check back into the Romantik Hotel. I will confront Frau Decker, letting her know we know she is the *Kommandant der Einheit*. And then we will see what unfolds."

"You and Lucinda will hold back but be there if or when needed. This has the potential to get nasty. The ledger listed twelve active cell members, any one of which may decide to take action."

"And when is this going down?" Lucinda asks.

"This afternoon."

After checking into the Romantik Hotel, Anderson finds Frau Decker in the lobby. As we are leaving, he turns to her and says, "Frau Decker, or is it Kommandant Decker? Perhaps if you have time, when we return from dinner, you can tell us about the boxcars."

She's left staring at Anderson as we walk out the door.

At the Gasthaus Zum Lindengarten we have a light dinner, a *Jagerschnitzel* for me and the house special, bratwurst and pomme frites, for Anderson.

All is going well until we leave. Exiting the Gasthaus, we are surprised by several men ... and the world goes dark!

15 Hospital

When I regain consciousness, I'm in a hospital room. Lucinda is there. "Where is Anderson?" I ask.

"He was in the van by the time we got there, and they were just about to throw you in. Seeing us, they dropped you and fled ... with Anderson. The local police were called; Henry is dealing with them now. They had you transported here."

My head was throbbing, and I was having difficulty focusing. "Where is here?" I managed to say.

"You are in the Zittau Regional Hospital. You have a bad concussion. The doctors want to keep you here for a day or two for observation."

As I drifted off, I said, "My wallet, card for Agent Hoffman, call her...."

I guess it was the next morning when I was conscious again. The nurse saw my eyes open. She called the resident doctor who shined lights in my eyes and asked how I felt in broken English.

"Like shit," I responded.

"Well, it sounds like he is back to normal," said Henry.

"When can I leave," I ask.

"We want to keep you for another day," said the doctor, "for observation."

As I started to get up, I was surprised to hear Gundi. "Stay put; there is nothing you can do now. But we can have a little talk. What happened?"

I'm reluctant to give her any information. "Look," she says, "I'm here unofficially. Rudolph wants to find his father, so work with me."

Okay, we have the same goal, rescuing Anderson. I told her the full story. I asked Lucinda for my phone. I retrieved the information Anderson, and I collected from the Eyeball cloud.

"*Heilige scheiße*," Gundi says as she flips through the data. "This is big!"

"Yes, but keep it quiet for now. There is a bigger target here, bringing down this Nazi cell."

"Okay, good point," Gundi says. "I'm going to give Frau Decker a visit."

"I'll go with you," Lucinda says. "Henry, you stay here with Sean."

Gundi is not happy with the company, but the two ladies leave together.

I decided to give Adam a call to update him. He and Henry have been on the phone throughout the night.

"Adam, Sean here. I'm fine, but the doc wants me to stay for another day. Anderson is still missing; we have a *Bundeskriminalamt* officer working with us. She's a friend of Andersons's son ... no, I'll fill you in later. She is working with us unofficially. I've asked her to keep it quiet until we get a lead on this group."

Andy said, "You had a call from a Colonel Emanual Castro in Argentina. He said you were asking about information on possible Nazi cells in Germany. He had three. I'm texting them to you." My phone dings as I thank Andy and disconnect.

I look at Andy's text. The second entry grabs my attention. *Loyale Bruderschaft.* They are located in Dresden. Dumberg's contact was Willie Broman, identified as the *Unterführer.*

16 First Contact

"Nice ride," says Lucinda trying to break the ice. Gundi is driving a red convertible, an Audi A5 Cabriolet.

Pulling up to the Romantik Hotel Gundi says, "Look, you're a guest here. Stand back and let me do my job. I get it that they are your friends, but I don't want to be worrying about you, so stay in the car."

As Gundi enters the hotel, she's followed by Lucinda. They find Frau Decker in the lobby.

"Where is Herr Anderson?" Gundi snaps.

Frau Decker looks at the two and tells them to get out.

Gundi pulls out her extendable baton, flicks it open, and whacks Decker on the left shin. Frau Deck crumples to the floor screaming in pain.

Gundi looks at Lucinda, "Well you're here; help me get her in that chair."

Once Frau Deck is sitting upright, Gundi asks again, "Where is Herr Anderson?" as she taps the injured shin with her baton. "I'll ask you one last time. This kneecap is my next target," tapping Decker's right leg.

She starts to answer between whimpers of pain when Carl and his two 'brownshirts' come in from the dining room. They see Decker in the chair and two women interrogating her; they attack.

Now that was probably not the smartest thing to do; get between two lethal females who were in the midst of a badass contest.

Lucinda took Carl out with a punch to his windpipe and as she swung around, delivered a well-aimed roundhouse kick to the first henchman's head. Gundi sidestepped the second henchman's full-body attack and helped him headfirst into the stone fireplace.

It was over in less than five seconds. "Not bad," said Gundi, eyeing Lucinda's work with some respect.

She turned back to Frau Decker, "You were about to say something."

Information started flowing. Anderson was being held in a Dresden warehouse owned by Willie Broman. There were probably two or three members of the *Loyale Bruderschaft*guarding him.

Gundi first called the local police to come and collect the four people she just arrested on assault and kidnapping charges. She then called her boss in Berlin and told him what she was into.

"This Nazi group appears to be headquartered in Dresden; a chapter is here in Jonsdorf. To make it more interesting, it appears the local chapter has been guarding Hitler's Treasure Train ... no it's not a myth. Herr Anderson found it. He's the one that has been kidnapped. I'm leaving for Dresden now. Isolate the building, but please wait until I get there."

"Sean asked you to keep a lid on that information!" said a fuming Lucinda.

"And who's going to get Anderson? We needed a rescue team. I got it!" Gundi shot back.

As they wait for the local police transport, Lucinda steps outside and calls Jacob. She updates him on what has transpired. "Anderson has been kidnapped, Sean is in the hospital with a concussion and Agent Hoffman, a condescending *Bundeskriminalamt* officer bitch is trying to sideline me. Since an American has been kidnapped, is there any way you can get me official standing here as an FBI rep?"

Four *Politzei* vehicles arrived, lights flashing. A small crowd gathers around the Romantik Hotel to watch the four, one a promenade member of the community who needs assistance from two officers, being perp-walked out of the hotel into the waiting vehicles.

"And I suppose you plan to come with me to Dresden?" says Gundi as the two get into her car.

Halfway to their destination, Gundi's boss calls. On the car's speakerphone, he tells her his boss just approved Lucinda Bjornsson's official standing; she's the FBI's rep on this case. "Play nice," were his last words as the call terminated.

"Bjornsson?" Gundi asks.

"Hafþór Júlíus Björnsson is my father, and yes, he is or was the holder of the 'World's Strongest Man' title. I'm surprised you recognized the name. No one in America knows him. And my mother is Theresa Evan, an Italian movie starlet from a bygone age."

"Theresa Evan. I watched her old movies when I was in college. I loved her," Gundi said. "Where are they now?"

"My mother didn't want to live in Iceland, and my father nixed Italy. They agreed on Copenhagen. Once 'we' get this cleaned up I plan to visit."

17 Dresden

The address Decker provided was an abandoned building located between *Strass des 17.Juni* and the railroad tracks. By the time Gundi and Lucinda arrived, the immediate area had been sealed by a special unit from the *Bundeskriminalamt,* with local police providing perimeter control.

Gundi's boss, Hans Schreiber was in charge. He waved them over to his command trailer. "Agent Björnsson, Jacob describes you as 'vengeance on legs' if I got the translation right, when on a mission."

"Let's just say I'm focused," said Lucinda. "Please call me Lucinda."

"Okay, well let's get to it. There has been no activity in the past two hours. Earlier, one man arrived, still inside. Our heat sensors indicate four bodies in the center of the building. We've inserted an optical cable and can see the kidnapped victim. He's tied to a chair … he's not going to last much longer. His three captors are about five meters away and appear to be sitting around a table. We delayed breaching the building until you arrived, but it's now 'game on.'"

Hans called his two squad leaders over, "On my command Team A will launch flash bangs and open the back wall with the armored breach vehicle. Team B will delay for ten seconds and quietly, if possible, force the front entrance and secure Herr Anderson.

"Go!" Hans yells into his mic. There is initial chaos, automatic weapons fired, and then silence. Lucinda and Gundi head for the front, the sliding door now off its track, Gundi in the lead with her sidearm drawn and Lucinda in her wake. They make it to Anderson who has just been cut free by an assault team member and is laid out on the floor, barely moving.

Gundi is on her intercom, "We need a med tech here now! Anderson is having difficulty breathing." Help arrives with no one paying much attention to the three bodies bleeding on the floor. The ambulance Hans had in reserve takes over. Anderson is on life support as it leaves the scene, headed for the hospital emergency room that Hans also had on standby.

Two of the captors are stabilized by Team A and follow Anderson to the hospital in a second ambulance. The third is dead.

Lucinda and Gundi rush to the hospital where a nurse intercepts them directing them to a small waiting room. "Your friend is in surgery. The doctor will be with you when he has finished," the nurse says as she leaves the room.

Lucinda calls Henry to get an update on Sean's condition and to tell him about Anderson. "He was barely breathing when we found him. He's in surgery right now ... I don't know; I haven't talked with the doctor yet." She disconnects after several more minutes.

"Well, how is Sean," Gundi asks.

"He's awake and insets on getting up. His first question was about Anderson."

Early that evening the doctor comes into the waiting room, "Your friend is out of danger. He had a collapsed lung, several broken ribs and was concussed. He took a brutal beating. He will not be able to leave the hospital for several days."

As the doctor is leaving, Lucinda is on her cell. "Henry, we just spoke with the doctor; Anderson is going to be fine but must remain in the hospital for the next few days. Tell Sean."

"Thanks for the news," says Sean who apparently has commandeered Henry's phone. "I discharged myself an hour ago. We are back in Jonsdorf at the Hotel Gondelfahrt. We are going to get a good night's sleep and then go on a 'Nazi hunt' in the morning."

Gundi, who is sitting next to Lucinda, interjects, "Don't do anything stupid. You have no authority here," she says into a disconnected phone.

Pulling out her cell Gundi calls her boss who is still at the crime scene. Putting him on the speaker, "Hans, Sean is up and has discharged himself from the hospital. He and Henry are in Jonsdorf and, I think, are planning on searching for other cell members. Should we get someone down there to assist?"

"Yes, we should and also secure that dairy barn until we can further investigate the supposed *Goldener Zug*. How long are you going to stay at the hospital? I could use you down there now."

"Anderson is stable; I'm on my way."

Lucinda, who has heard the entire conversation, is ripped between going with Gundi or waiting in the recovery room for Anderson.

Gundi solves her dilemma. "You should be here when Anderson wakes up. I'll arrange a ride for you in the morning. Nothing is going to happen in Jonsdorf tonight."

18 The Dairy Barn

Sean and Henry are seated in the hotel's small restaurant waiting for their order to be served, Sean with his trademark cup of coffee. Henry is asking what the plan is for the morning.

As Sean starts to lay out the day's plan, "I think we should start with Herr Nicholas's dairy barn. We need to secure the ledger..." trailing off as Gundi walks in.

"Excellent idea," says Gundi. My boss, Agent Schreiber, has ordered me to secure the dairy barn and whatever evidence it may contain. My team will be arriving in a couple of hours."

"As for you two, I have two alternatives. I'll arrest you if you don't stand down, or we work together. Your choice."

After a moment's hesitation and a side glance at Henry, Sean says, "Okay, what do you want us to do?"

"Good choice," said Gundi. "Lucinda will join us later after Anderson is awake. Anderson, by the way, came out of surgery at ten last night. He had a collapsed lung, several broken ribs, and numerous contusions. With a little hospital rest, he is expected to make a full recovery."

Who took him?" asks Sean.

"We think it was the *Loyale Bruderscha*. Willie Broman was named by Frau Decker. Anderson was being held in one of his warehouses."

At the mention of Broman's name, Sean speaks up. "You recall I told you about finding Nazi gold in Argentina a few years ago; my Argentine contact, Colonel Castro, confiscated *Adler Bruderschaft*'s records. Three sister groups were identified in Germany, one in Dresden, the *Loyale Bruderscha*; Willie Broman, its leader."

"And to answer your earlier question, yes, the Mossad took all the gold. It was donated to a holocaust survivors' support group."

"While we wait for your team, I suggest we secure Nicholas's dairy barn and get the ledger."

"My thoughts," said Gundi. You know the way; I'll follow you."

As the three approached the barn, an elderly man came out holding a shotgun. "Get off my property!" he is shouting.

Gundi holds up her warrant, "I'm Agent Hoffman with the *Bundeskriminalamt*. Put down that shotgun before things get ugly."

With great reluctance Nicholas lowers the gun; Henry walks forward and takes it from his hands.

"Herr Nicholas we would like to inspect your ban. Will you join us?" Gundi said not as a question but as a command.

They walk through the barn to a small hidden door in the back. Henry has taken up a position in the back of Herr Nicholas to discourage him from bolting.

As Anderson opens the door and steps in, he asks, "Where is the light switch?"

72

Reluctantly Nicholas steps in, to the right, and flips the switch.

As Gundi looks around, she is saying under her breath, *"Heilige scheiße."*

The room is about ten by fifteen meters in size. A large conference table in the middle. Hitler's portrait is on the far wall. The membership ledger is directly beneath it on a makeshift altar. There are large Nazi swastika banners on each wall.

"Come over here," Sean says as he pulls back the corner of one of the banners on the far wall revealing a small door. He opens the door, but beyond the threshold, it is utterly black. He returns to the altar where he finds matches beside the two candles. With lit candles, he leads the group into the tunnel. There are only a few meters between the crude wooden wall and the front of the boxcar. Gundi tries to slip between the boxcar and the tunnel wall, but it's too tight.

"Anderson and I had to crawl under the side of the boxcar to get here. There are four boxcars. It's passable most of the way once you get beyond this point." He goes on to tell Gundi how they found the back entrance.

Back in the dairy barn portion of the structure, Gundi is telling Nicholas he is under arrest for harboring Nazi sympathizers.

Sean chimes in, "I think he's one of the sympathizers; he's listed as a member on page two of the ledger."

When Gundi's team arrives at the barn, she has them take Nicholas into custody.

"What about my cows," Nicholas is yelling.

"What about them," Gundi answers.

"Who's going to milk them? You?"

73

"Shit," says Gundi. "What do you suggest?"

"Turn me loose!"

"Not going to happen."

"Let me call my cousin then. He has a dairy farm."

Later that morning Gundi is on the phone with Agent Schreiber, "Boss, the gold train is here; I've seen it, I've touched it. We also got the local *Loyale Bruderschaft*chapter's membership ledger. I'd like to start pulling these people in."

"Secure the site until we get the proper people there. As for arrests, hold off until I get there. Oh, and by the way Lucinda will be working with the team up here for a few days," Agent Schreiber said leaving a puzzled Gundi.

19 Willie Broman

Early that morning Anderson woke. Lucinda was sitting, more accurately sleeping, in the chair with her feet propped on the second chair. "Where am I?" he croaks waking Lucinda up.

She's up and gives him a sip of water before answering. "You're in a Dresden hospital. The *Bundeskriminalamt* rescued you yesterday. Three days ago, Frau Decker had the *Loyale Bruderschaft*kidnap you. Henry and I were able to save Sean. You were already in the van. Sean spent a day in a hospital in Zittau with a concussion. He checked himself out yesterday evening. He and Henry are now on a Nazi Hunt in Jonsdorf. Gundi is on her way to join them. The doctor says you will be here for a few days."

"I feel like shit," Anderson says.

"And you look like shit," said Agent Schreiber. "I'm Gundi's boss, Hans Schreiber. Agent Hoffman has been telling me about you and what you found or think you have found. She and your people are investigating as we speak."

Turning to Lucinda, "Gundi promised to get you down to Jonsdorf later today," said Agent Schreiber. "I have an alternative for you. You have official status here. Would you consider joining my team as Gundi's replacement? We are taking down Willie Broman. He's the one who caused your friend to be in this condition."

"A fully functioning member?"

"Yes."

"Okay, I'm on board," says Lucinda. She turns to Anderson, "I'll check back in later."

As Agent Schreiber starts to leave the room, Anderson says, "You know with Lucinda on your team this Broman character will be lucky to come out of this alive."

Walking out of the hospital Schreiber says, "You can ride with me back to headquarters, and we will get you outfitted."

At headquarters Agent Schreiber introduces Lucinda to his team. "Lucinda is a highly decorated FBI agent and will be an asset in taking down this *Loyale Bruderschaft*cell. Manfred, please take her under your wing and get her outfitted."

Lucinda, do you have a preference for a weapon? Our standard issue is the MP4."

"That works for me," she responds.

"Okay, we move out within the hour. Let's get it together team," Schreiber says with some enthusiasm.

As the team prepares to load into the two SWAT vehicles Agent Schreiber gets an urgent call. "*Geschissen!*" he yells. "A local police lieutenant, seeking glory, launched a preemptive raid on Willie's compound. There are two dead officers and a third seriously injured they can't get to. Okay, team, buckle up; we're going into a live firefight!"

The two vehicles crash the main gate to the compound. The local police are hunkered down exchanging fire with Broman's men. There is now a large Nazi battle flag flying over the house.

"It doesn't look like they plan to surrender," said Schreiber as the two vehicles disgorged their cargo. "Pair up," he orders. "Manfred you with Lucinda."

Schreiber sends two of the five pairs to retrieve the injured officer. After consulting a map of the compound, he deploys the other three teams directing two to breach the main house and Rudi and Lucinda to secure the back.

The pairs disperse, Manfred and Lucinda reaching the back of the house as gunfire explodes at the front. The armored SWAT vehicles move closer laying down deadly fire.

As the two take up positions, no one exits from the back. Manfred is hit as gunfire erupts from Lucinda's left. Two figures coming out of the hedge are on Lucinda before she can get her rifle up. From reflex, she flips the first. He ends up with his leg impaled on a waist-high ornamental wrought iron fence, the kind with spikes on the top. As he's dangling there, the second attacker is on Lucinda with a wicked-looking knife. She fends off his first strike, and then they are both on the ground, Lucinda on the bottom.

As the gunfire subsides, voices can be heard inside the house ordering people to the floor. Apparently, Willie's men weren't prepared to follow him to Valhalla.

Schreiber called in several ambulances, the first for the wounded officer that the team was able to rescue. The second was for one of the *Bundeskriminalamt* members who was shot in the leg. The

77

wounded *Loyale Bruderschaft*members were transported by rescue vehicles under guard.

Agent Schreiber was speechless when he came out the back door. The first thing he saw was a bloody Lucinda. "Are you wounded?" were his first panicked words.

"It's his blood," Lucinda said as she pointed to a body with the knife protruding from the chest. Schreiber then noticed Lucinda's impaled attacker on the fence. It took three agents to lift him, painfully, off the fence.

Later according to Manfred, as Lucinda pushed the attacker off her, the body rolled over, and Manfred saw the knife firmly implanted in his chest.

Manfred was fine except for badly bruised ribs; his bulletproof vest worked. As Schreiber walked Manfred back to the men congregating around the vehicles, Manfred was heard saying, "She was like a reborn Brunhilda."

20 Nazi Hunt

Agent Schreiber was waiting for Lucinda to emerge from the dressing room. "You're looking much better without all that blood. Congratulations on a job well done. Your actions saved Manfred's life."

"I'm headed to the hospital. I need to get a statement from Anderson. Do you want a ride?"

At the hospital, they find a middle-aged man sitting with Anderson. Anderson introduces him, "This is my son Rudolph. Gundi told him I was here."

Schreiber steps forward to shake his hand, saying, "I am glad you are here; family is always good in the healing process."

Lucinda, on the other hand is holding back wondering who this guy is. Anderson never talked about a son in Germany.

"Lucinda," Anderson calls out, "Don't be bashful; Rudi won't bite. It's a long story, and I'm not going into it now; Sean can give you the details."

"Herr Anderson, I need to get a statement from you. I can come back later."

"We can do it now. I'm leaving Dresden in the morning. Rudi made arrangements for me at a private hospital in Munich. Then I will be staying at his home to recuperate ... giving me a chance to get to know his wife and my granddaughter. Let's do my statement while Rudi and Lucinda go get coffee."

When Rudi and Lucinda return, Agent Schreiber is just finishing up his paperwork.

"Agent Schreiber," Rudi starts. "I believe my father, or more accurately his company Eyeball Inc. is due the finder's fee for recovered Nazi loot. Ten percent of the total value, isn't it?"

"Yes, but that's handled by another government department."

He turns to Lucinda, "I'm headed to Jonsdorf in the morning. With Anderson's departure tomorrow, you'll be rejoining your friends. Would you like a ride to Jonsdorf?"

***

The following afternoon Lucinda takes the last room in the Hotel Gondelfahrt. The *Bundeskriminalamt* have made the hotel their base of operations. The owners, a young couple, are thrilled at the prospect of a 'full house' for the next few weeks."

Agent Schreiber's first order of business is to see the boxcars for himself. Sean is the guide. The rest follow the two to the dairy barn; it's only a short walk from the hotel.

Schreiber's first comment was the same as Gundi's, *"Heilige scheiße."*

"I need to call Berlin; a proper recovery team is needed down here. This will be a several-week project."

80

"Gundi, you said you have a list of local Nazis. Let's pick them up. Lucinda, you'll join us?"

For the rest of the week, other local members of the *Loyale Bruderscha's* local chapter are tracked down. The mayor, the postmaster, and three other promenade community leaders. Also netted is the owner of the café we first stopped at, Gertrude's employer. The two most committed members flee to Prague resulting in an Interpol warrant for their arrest.

At week's end we gather at the café, and Gertrude, in normal dress, serves our orders. "Your arrest of the old fart was a blessing. All that pompous ass did was harangue customers about the 'good old days.' His son now runs the café and bakery. Business has doubled," she says.

"The *Bundeskriminalamt's* business in Jonsdorf is concluded," said Schreiber. The recovery team will be here for the next few weeks.

"Gundi and I are going back to Berlin. Lucinda, I'll be telling Jacob you exceeded his description of you. If you ever get bored with the FBI, I can find a space for you."

"Sean, I understand you are staying in Germany to oversee 'our' recovery efforts, guarding your 10 percent I suppose. If the tale is correct and there are over three hundred tons of gold, Eyeball is looking at 10 percent of over a trillion euros. I predict a long-drawn-out legal fight. If I can be of any help, call me."

"Henry and I are going home tomorrow," Lucinda said. "We've got some unfinished business with a cartel child smuggling ring. Chloe's last email said they have a handle on the ringleaders."

81

"Gundi, it's been fun; if you ever decide to visit the States, let me know. I'll give you a personal tour of the FBI."

21　P Contest

Representatives from the *Bundesamt für Kriegsvernichtung*, the German Office of War Recovery, take control of the site as the *Bundeskriminalamt's* people depart. As word of Hitler's *Goldener Zug* leaks out, there is concern about looters. Nicholas's dairy farm is locked down.

The *Bundesamt für Kriegsvernichtung's* team leader is a weaselly little man named Walter Heimer. Hans Schreiber made a point of introducing me to him and establishing my interest in the site.

Walter was all smiles until the next morning when he ordered me off the site. "Herr Murphy, you have no authority to be here. If you persist in trespassing on this recovery site, I will have you arrested."

"What do you mean I have no authority? Under German law, my employer Eyeball owns 10 percent of this."

"That's debatable," said Walter as he pulled out his cell phone. "Leave before I call the police to have you removed."

Sitting in the café, I'm fuming. I decided to call Anderson to share my frustration. After relating my tale, "Sean, don't do anything rash. I have an idea. I'll call you back."

An hour later Anderson calls and puts Rudi on the line. "Sean, Rudi here. I'll meet you at Anderson's favorite Jonsdorf café at three tomorrow. In the interim, stay away from the dairy farm."

I'm intrigued; what does Rudi have up his sleeve? I normally distrust lawyers; I usually end up losing.

I'm at the café by two thirty, Gertrude commenting on my frequent visits, "Our coffee is good, but is it that good?" she says with a laugh as she slips me an unordered *Berliner*.

At three, like clockwork, Rudi drives up in his Mercedes. "Hop in, Sean; we have people to see."

Our first stop is the town center where he picks up Officer Scholtz. Scholtz, a member of Zittau's police force. He is assigned to Jonsdorf to provide a local police presence. Scholtz is expecting us and gets in.

The three of us drive over to the recovery site, driving into the middle of the activity.

Walter Heimer sees me as I get out of the car and makes a beeline to me. "I warned you!" he stammers. "Who's this, your lawyer? I'm going to have you all arrested."

He doesn't notice Officer Scholtz until the police officer gets out of the back of the Mercedes.

Scholtz walks over to Walter and without a word, hands him papers.

"What's this?"

"It's a Cease Work Order from the Federal Court. No further recovery work is to be carried out on this site without a representative from Kirkland & Ellis International. One more shovel in the ground, I'll arrest you."

Walter is looking at the papers in his hand as Rudi says, "Cheer up Walter, I'm a lawyer with Kirkland & Ellis International. I'm here to solve your problem," as he hands Walter another piece of paper.

Rudi continues, "That paper you're trying to ignore names my firm's official representative, the person that will be monitoring your recovery efforts for my client."

Walter's eyes skim the latest piece of paper, he sees my name, Sean Murphy. It's obvious Walter is rattled. "Any questions," Rudi asks.

"I'll make a space for him in the tent; he can watch from there," Walter says.

"Not good enough Walter," says Rudi. "If you read the Cease Work Order, my representative is to have unrestricted access to the recovery site. He can watch everything you do. And to make myself clear," Rudi says with a threatening voice, "he can monitor you taking a crap in the site's portapotty if he wishes."

***

After our initial kerfuffle, Walter got on with his work, for the most part ignoring my presence. His work crew emptied the barn, boxed up all the Nazi paraphilia, and oversaw the removal of the dairy equipment. That equipment and the cows were transported over to Nicolus's cousin. The barn was then bulldozed, and all the rubble cleared from the site. All that was left was the crude wooden wall covering the entrance to the tunnel.

When they were ready to take down that wall, some bigwigs from Berlin were on-site to witness the re-emergence of the *Goldener Zug* after close to eighty years of being hidden in a mountain.

The bulldozer had a chain strung through the wall. On Walter's signal, it rolled forward, bringing down the wall. It was somewhat of an anticlimax. All that could be seen was the front end of a boxcar in a gloomy cave.

Given the tight fit of the boxcars in the tunnel, it was decided to lay fifty meters of track to allow the four boxcars to be pulled out into sunlight.

22 Recovery

Over the next week, fifty meters of track were laid across the former dairy pasture. The new track was linked to the old tracks. Armed guards were posted at the mouth of the tunnel. Our rear entrance had been dynamited, collapsing the side tunnel. Lighting worthy of a major sporting venue was erected resulting in complaints from the local populace. There was not much for me to do other than watch the workmen. Walter Heimer and I developed a relationship, one of mutual indifference.

As work progressed, Berlin bigwigs announced the finding of Hitler's Treasure Train and that its unveiling to the public would be in ten days. The event would be broadcast live by all regional public-service broadcasters. Major media news outlets, *Die Welt*, *Bild*, etc., were invited. Due to security concerns, the general public would not be allowed on-site.

The day of the unveiling was a bright, crisp fall day. Bleachers, erected for the event, were filling up. Cars bringing the invited dignitaries were parked at the far end of the old pasture, giving it the look of a used car lot. Television crews were jockeying for camera positions. The drone of generators, although muffled, could be heard.

I had a group of seats reserved, over Walter's objections, for the Eyeball contingent. The show was scheduled to start at noon. At eleven thirty the Anderson Party arrived. Anderson was now mobile, almost back to normal. As expected, Rudi was with him, and to my surprise, Freddy followed behind. "Colonel, what is Freddy doing here?" I asked.

"I believe Freddy has a vested interest in this," he responded. "It will also give Major Freedman some exposure for future business opportunities."

At noon sharp, one has to credit the Germans for maintaining a schedule; the Director for the *Bundesamt für Kriegsvernichtung* took the mike. "Thank you all for your interest. This is a momentous day. For years the legend of Hitler's Treasure Train has circulated. We all thought it was a myth, myself included. In a few minutes, those two bulldozers will pull the four boxcars out of that tunnel to this space directly in front of us. Work crews will then open the cars. Recovery specialists will make an initial assessment of the contents. They are wearing cameras. We have a Wi-Fi link you can tap into so you can see everything the specialists see. That link is posted at the base of the podium."

The Director gave the signal, the bulldozers started moving forward. In typical German thoroughness, the wheels of the boxcars had been lubricated earlier in the week, and tests conducted to ensure they weren't frozen by eighty years of rust.

As the boxcars came to a rest, thirty meters in front of the audience, workmen moved to the lead boxcar, positioned a platform by the sliding door, and broke the Wehrmacht seal. Recovery specialists then mounted the platform and pushed open the door.

88

The interior was full. Two specialists gently removed the first box. Prying it open they found a Renoir painting of a young woman. The next five boxes contained paintings by other masters.

Walter positioned shipping containers off to one side, where the boxcar contents were temporally stored by museum curators. Two containers were close to full when the lead recovery specialist announced that all the small crates had been opened; all that remained were what looked to be munition storage boxes. With some trepidation, they popped the lid of one; the content was gold bullion bars. The bars were all uniform in size, stamped with a swastika, and guessed to weigh over ten kilos each.

The second boxcar was similar to the first. The only exception was the five Greek statues, each about the size of a man.

The recovery experts estimated that the first two boxcars contained over seventy-five tons of gold, each. If the last two cars contained similar amounts, the mythical three hundred-plus tons of gold would be realized.

We were now into late afternoon when the Director reclaimed the microphone. "Guests, this has been an amazing day. Some of the art we found was believed to have been destroyed in the war. It will be evaluated and cataloged by our specialists. As for the gold, what can I say? I'm speechless."

"We are going to call it quits for today, saving the last two cars for tomorrow. We will start at ten. Please vacate the area in an orderly fashion. Our guards will soon be securing the site."

As we were preparing to leave, two of the major newspapers approached Anderson. "We understand that you discovered the treasure train. Can you give us the story?"

"No," said the Colonel, "but I'll sell it to you. This is my attorney, Rudolph Zimmerman," he said, indicating Rudi. Talk to him.

"We understand you have Goebbels's diary. The diary that led you here. Will you make that diary public?" said the second journalist.

"Again no, that diary belongs to Major Freedman," said Anderson pointing to Freddy. But for today, please direct your inquiries to my attorney who is also representing Major Freedman.

23 Post Recovery

At the end of the second day, there were eight shipping containers loaded with paintings and statutes. The contents of each container were photographed and cataloged. I insisted on copies. Walter was resistant, but Rudi's stare quieted him. The containers were loaded onto flatbeds. That evening a convoy of eight trucks and four police cars left Jonsdorf and headed to a warehouse on the Berlin outskirts where the disposition of the contents would occur, most likely a several-year process.

The *Goldener Zug* legend had three hundred thirty tons of gold on the train. As it turned out the number of tons was about right, but they were metric tonnes, about 10 percent heavier than English ton. There were three hundred 'munition' boxes in each car, each box containing twenty gold bars and weighing a little over two hundred seventy kilograms each or six hundred pounds.

As we were leaving, I had one last shot at Walter. "Walter, we'll take those thirty boxes as our 10 percent finder's fee. We'll pick them up in the morning."

The poor guy, face turning red, sputters, "I'll see you in hell first!"

Rudi chuckling, says, "I've heard court called many things, but that is an upgrade."

We are spending one last night in Jonsdorf. I suggest a beer or two at the Gasthaus Zum Lindengarten. Winking at Anderson, "Don't get yourself kidnapped again."

Several of the locals thank us for getting rid of Carl and his goons. "They've ridden roughshod over us for years. Them and the corrupt town officials."

The locals then share some of the local legends about the war years, visits by Nazi leaders, treasures hidden in the mountain, and the not-so-secret *Loyale Bruderscha* cell. The one surprise was Frau Decker's role.

We are up early the next morning. Anderson insists on stopping at 'his' café. Gertrude is there, leaving me wondering if the poor lady ever had any time off.

"Gertrude, when we first met you, you said nothing ever happened here. I hope we livened it up for you," said Anderson. "Your mother saw the train go through town; now you've seen it come out of hiding. I doubt if I will ever be this way again. I wish you well."

***

Back in Munich, in Kirkland & Ellis International's conference room, Rudi is telling us where we are.

"Let me address the easy things first. Major Freedman has retained me to handle the sale of Goebbels's diary. I advised an online auction. It would get the most coverage and worldwide attention. He agreed. The auction will be held just after the National Geographic documentary is released this winter. The one caveat, he retains his publication rights."

"Your agreement with Freddy gives him 10 percent of the gross proceeds Eyeball realizes. This is where it gets difficult. That brings me to the value of the gold. It is in the trillions. First, the exact amount fluctuates daily.

"Second, if all the gold recovered is put on today's market, it would have the same result as Mansa Moussa's pilgrimage to Mecca in 1324. Moussa was a Mali sultan. He took so much gold from Timbuktu and was so generous with it that he devalued Egypt's economy for the following decade.

"Third, who are the rightful owners of the gold? East European countries are already clamoring for the return of the gold looted by the occupying Germans. I think the International Court of Justice in The Hague will agree with them.

"To put it more succinctly, this will be tied up in the court for the next decade ... or longer. I suggest we propose an early settlement. How does five billion euros sound?"

"I agree," said Anderson, "but let's start at ten. That gives us a little room to negotiate."

"Now for the art, it's handled by a different branch of the government," said Rudi. "They want to return the pieces to the rightful owners as quickly as possible and are most eager to settle any finder's fee claims. The problem is valuation. Most of the pieces are priceless; identified as national treasures."

The head curator at the Academy of the Arts Museum in Berlin places a value of fifty to one hundred million euros if the pieces were to be auctioned off. The chief curator at the Louvre suggests Otto is smoking weed again, giving an estimate of twice that.

93

"I've been told that if you are receptive, they will pay, immediately, five million as a finder's fee."

"Can I make a suggestion? We take the five million and give it to Gundi."

With a puzzled look, Anderson asks, "Why?"

"Gundi confided to Lucinda that her grandfather was a Jew who died in one of the camps," I said. "Her grandmother, a non-Jew, and Gundi's mother were ostracized during the war years, only surviving on the goodwill of others. Over the years Gundi has been a supporter of holocaust survivor groups here in Germany. I suggest we assign the finder's fee to Gundi with the stipulation that it be used to support these groups in any manner she finds appropriate."

"That's a noble thought Sean," said Rudi. "If I didn't know better, I'd think you were a lawyer. Giving up a small amount for a potentially much bigger payout, and as a side benefit a positive bump in public opinion."

"Okay, make it happen," says Anderson.

We spent the next week in Munich tying up loose ends. There were a few interviews, mostly with print journalists but one on live television. An attractive female TV anchor who quickly succumbed to Anderson's charm.

We had plane reservations for later that week when both Anderson and I received Andy's urgent text message, "SARAH IS MISSING!"

24 Missing

No sooner had we read Andy's text than Anderson's cell rang; Andy was calling. Anderson engaged the phone's speaker so I could hear.

"Anderson, bad news, is Sean there?"

"I'm here," I said. "What about Sarah!"

"Chloe and Sarah are working with the FBI on the cartel's child smuggling ring. They think they have a handle on the ringleaders, apparently in the Wilmington area. Sarah, Chloe, and Butch went to the Eastern Shore to investigate rumors of immigrant child labor being used on the produce farms.

"Sarah was snatched from the motel last night. There was a running gunfight; Chloe killed one of the abductors. Butch gave up the chase when Chloe was hit. Sarah was gone by the time he got Chloe stabilized. Chloe was hit in the shoulder; she will recover. She's in Dover's regional hospital.

"Jacob is pulling out all stops to rescue one of the Bureau's former agents."

"We should be home tomorrow; I'll find a flight for tonight," said Anderson.

"Don't bother," said Andy, "I've sent the Eyeball Gulfstream to Munich. It will be there in three hours."

***

We're landing at Richmond International Airport as the sun is rising. We left Munich late last night and spent the night in the air with little sleep. Adam is there in the baggage claim area.

"Sean, I'm sorry, there is nothing new to report. Jacob's people have swarmed the State. Delaware is not that big; they'll find something."

"How's Chloe? Asks Anderson.

"The surgeon was happy with the surgery's results. Chloe will make a full recovery. The bullet just hit muscle in her shoulder. At worst, she will have a scar."

"Let's get to the office," Anderson said.

Sitting at his desk, the first thing Anderson did was call Jacob. "What can Eyeball do to help in the search?" he asks.

"Sit tight," Jacob said; "the Bureau has a full-court press looking for Sarah. We gathered the surveillance tapes from the motel and the gas station across the street. Lucinda is screening them as we speak."

Fifteen minutes later Jacob calls back, "Anderson, we got the abduction on tape. A dark-colored, late model minivan with Mayland tags."

"Can you get the plate number?"

"Yes. We've passed it on to the Delaware State Police and State Police in the surrounding states," Said Jacob. "They have an eighteen-hour head start, but we will find them."

"Guys, there is nothing we can do right now. I suggest we get cleaned up, have breakfast, and if possible, a little shuteye. We need to be ready to go when we have something to act on," said Henry.

"He's right," said Anderson. "We need to treat this as a combat mission; make use of downtime."

Anderson sent his secretary out for three large takeouts from the Waffle House. While waiting for her return, we washed up and got a change of clothes from our go bags.

Two hours later Jacob's call found me stretched out on the sofa in the lobby as Anderson was yelling, "Sean, Henry, let's go Jacobe found the vehicle."

We're in Eyeball's parking lot waiting.

"What are we waiting for?" I ask. "What did Jacob find?"

"The minivan was spotted in Wilmington. His people are sealing the area. Jacob is sending a helicopter for us," Anderson is saying as we hear our ride approaching.

As it sets down, we see that Jacob and Lucinda are in the chopper. We scramble abroad and grab the headsets Jacob is pointing at. Anderson hangs back, "You three go; I'll stay here by the phone. This past month has taken a toll … I'm not as young as I use to be."

As the chopper lifts off, Jacob is saying, "We think we have them cornered in an abandoned industrial complex in Wilmington."

25 Rescue

The Feds had the minivan bottled up in an old industrial site. This was preceded by a car chase through downtown Wilmington where several cars were sideswiped by the fleeing vehicle before it swerved into the abandoned lot and found there were no exits.

The senior police officer on the scene reported to the FBI agents that two occupants fled into the abandoned plant. The agents requested that the local police establish a perimeter while they waited for the Agent in Charge. Jacob's arrival superseded the AIC's control of the situation.

Jacob wanted to hold back, waiting for additional men, when the Eyeball team, with Lucinda in tow, preempted Jacob and rushed the old building. I directed Lucinda to stay with me as we moved into the first-floor space. Butch and Henry headed to the second floor.

As Lucinda and I rounded a large piece of equipment, she motioned me to stop and pointed to the far corner of the work area. Behind some old machines, we found two men hiding. They weren't cartel soldiers; they weren't armed. They were scared shitless.

Lucinda grabbed the one who appeared to be in charge. "Where is the lady you kidnapped!!" she yelled.

As he started to deny any kidnapping, Lucinda 'bitch slapped' him twice. His eyeballs were rattling in their sockets like a pinball machine.

"I'll ask you one last time," she said.

"We were told to take her to the port and drop her off at the Esmeralda."

"The Esmeralda?" I asked.

"A small cargo ship docked by the Dole Fresh Fruit warehouse," he answered, cringing back from Lucinda.

We turned the two over to Jacob's people. With Jacob's help, we commandeered an FBI vehicle and led a convoy of Feds to the city's dock area.

We found the Esmeralda, a Panamanian Flagged cargo ship. As cargo ships go, this one was small. Jacob led his team up the gangplank. We followed. Most of the crew and officers were off the ship. The chief mate in charge briefly tried to keep us from boarding. Jacob was having none of that and motioned to one of his agents to arrest him if he continued impeding the FBI.

"Where is the lady that was brought on board earlier?" Anderson asked.

Nervously looking around the man said they were holding her in the crew's quarters.

After getting directions, we were off. In the crew's galley, we surprised the three abductors and had them in zip ties by the time Jacob got there.

"Where is the lady!" I yelled.

No answer, just smirks.

"Jacob, can you give me a few minutes with them?"

Now Butch was in the Special Forces and had served in Afghanistan. Henry, on the other hand, was a Navy SEAL.

"Butch, remember how we got the Taliban to talk? Let's show Henry. Which one should we start with?"

Butch points to the more defiant one. He and I lifted him by his arms and dragged him into an adjacent room and shut the door.

For the next ten minutes, Henry hears a body hitting the wall, loud cries of pain, screams, and yelling. When Butch and I emerge, covered in blood, I say, "That was one tough bastard. Did you see his face when I did him? Butch, where did you learn that trick? From the Taliban?"

"Okay, the next one," I say as I grab the one who looks weakest of the remaining two. "Where's the lady?"

He's stuttering as Butch, and I start dragging him out.

"She's in the last cabin on this deck," he stutters in fear.

"It's not often we get uncoerced answers," Jacob says with a smile.

I rush down the passageway, find the cabin, and there is Sarah, hog-tied, lying on the bunk. I cut her free and hugged her. "I've got you."

I helped her to her feet, a few more hugs, and then we moved down the passageway back to the galley. Butch and Henry were retrieving the man we had just brutalized. His mouth was still sealed with duck tape, but otherwise, unharmed.

His two companions looked on in some amazement, thinking he was dead. Jackob is laughing. "My throat still hurts from all that screaming," said Butch.

"Where did the blood come from?" asks Lucinda.

"It's from my arm," I said, raising it to show the makeshift bandage.

Sarah sees him, walks over, and delivers a solid blow to his nose. Blood erupts from his nostrils. We watched him flop around on the floor. Jacob finally says, "Get the tape off his mouth before he drowns in his own blood."

26 Debrief

A few days later Jacob is visiting Eyeball. Anderson is back to his old self; a few days' rest does wonders. And if I'm honest, I'm also feeling better. I'm no spring chicken.

"Sean," Jacob starts, "you have an interesting integration technique."

"I learned that from you. Remember when we questioned the mafia foot soldiers when we were taking down their financial empire?"

"Don't know a thing about it," said the smiling agent. "But a piece of good news, with a little pressure, our arrestees gave up their cartel boss. A sleazeball living in Miami, Padro Fernandez. He's been on our radar for years, but nothing ever tied back to him. As we speak, Lucinda is executing a search warrant on his home and office. Under our contract with Eyeball, I sent Henry with her for support."

"How is Chloe?" Jacob asks Anderson.

"She's been released from the hospital and is staying with Sarah."

"They were both at S&C INVESTIGATIVE SERVICES this morning," I said. "I asked Sarah to take some time off, but…"

***

After Anderson treated everyone to lunch, Jacob headed back to the Hoover Building; Butch, Anderson, and I headed back to Anderson's office where Anderson said he had a surprise waiting.

Walking into the building, who do we find sitting in the lobby, Freddy? Anderson herded us into the conference room, ensuring I had my cup of coffee.

"I invited Freddy to join us this afternoon. We have unfinished business."

"Early yesterday Rudolph called to get my blessings on our final settlement with the *Bundesamt für Kriegsvernichtung*. As you know, they first proposed five billion euros. I asked Rudi to counteroffer with ten billion. They came back at six with a promise of a quick settlement. I told Rudi to accept. Funds will be transferred by the end of next week. Since we had no contract with them, Rudi felt a five hundred-million-euro fee for Kirkland & Ellis was fair."

"Eyeball's net is €5,500,000,000, or $6,037,350,000 at the current exchange rate. Our deal with Freddy gives him 10 percent of our net. So, Freddy, we owe you a little over six hundred million dollars."

I look over at him; he's in a state of shock. "What am I going to do with all that money?" he murmurs.

"Get yourself an investment adviser; don't drink it," says Anderson. "I can make some recommendations."

"As for you Sean, I can upgrade your desk," said a laughing Anderson. "Don't worry; you and Henry will be taken care of."

"We should set aside a little something for Lucinda, but her being a federal agent makes it a little more difficult. What would you say if we set aside ten million and gave it to her parents to hold in trust for her? Jacob has no problem with this."

"Have you told her?" I asked.

"Not yet. But I have one twist. I propose we have Gundi deliver the news to her parents … as a reward for her help. I know she is in awe of Lucinda's father and is a fan of her mother's movies. This would give her a chance to meet them."

"Neat idea," I say, "but tell Lucinda first."

***

It's now a few weeks later, and Sarah and I are snuggled up on her couch, Sparkles lying between us.

"You and Chloe are a success; S&C INVESTIGATIVE SERVICES brought down a child smuggling ring and helped dismantle a cartel enterprise," I say while sipping my beer. "I now have a few dollars set aside. Will you marry me?"

The poor lady almost chokes on her wine hearing my question.

End

www.ingramcontent.com/pod-product-compliance
Lightning Source LLC
Chambersburg PA
CBHW020140150626
46552CB00021B/1009